DESERT ASCENT

Desert Ascent

or

A Brief History of Eternity

Simon Parke

Hodder & Stoughton
LONDON SYDNEY AUCKLAND

First published in Great Britain 1997

10 9 8 7 6 5 4 3 2

British Library Cataloguing in Publication Data:
A record for this book is available from the British Library.

ISBN 0 340 69397 5

Typeset in Monotype Columbus by
Strathmore Publishing Services, London N7.

Printed and bound in Great Britain by
Caledonian International Book Manufacturing Ltd, Glasgow

Hodder and Stoughton Ltd
A division of Hodder Headline PLC
338 Euston Road, London NW1 3BH

to my mother and father
who, one sunny afternoon in an
English country garden, listened
for the songs sung to them in
their cradles

to Rowena and Andrew who walked
a field with me as we listened to
the songs sung to us

respect, love and thanks

Contents

An Introduction

JUST occasionally it happens. Just occasionally, that manuscript from heaven appears. It excites. It places deep within the very marrow of the soul a rich and enduring rainbow of hope.

This isn't that manuscript. But then again, it's extraordinary what different people can find buried within the least promising of land. And anyway, I need the money frankly ...

The writer is an abbot of dubious repute, who you may or may not warm to. (Since starting work on the editing I've actually discovered he lives very near to me, but we haven't met, and I think I feel I want to keep it that way.) Fortunately though, he doesn't fill the canvas, and it's not impossible that you'll be able to pour yourself into the spaces beyond – for in the desert the horizons are broad and the paths across it, enjoyably, if somewhat worryingly trackless.

Mary Gibson, Rachel Montgomery, Jez Todd and

Angela Reith have all read the manuscript at various stages, for which the reader should be very grateful. And Judith Longman has been a persistent, encouraging and spacious presence in the tedious business of editing yet more ramblings from the desert.

Joy, Chloe, Harry and Syd have lived with me throughout – the hardest calling of all.

Abbot Peter provides his own prologue. So enjoy. And in the meantime, eternity. And maybe one day, that manuscript …

S. P.

All Saints' Day, 1996

Prologue

A bishopric or sex? Given the option, which would I choose? I discovered my preference in the desert. Not that it had been a particularly pressing issue in my life. But it's strange what the desert search throws up along the way. In fact, I'd been looking for a ladder at the time. But I'm jumping ahead. Because obviously that's Stage Four. Stage Four of the process is not being able to find the ladder. Anywhere. Any sort. No ladders for love or money. Thank you and goodnight. Well, it's obvious. But then I was there. And I was the one who cracked ...

But of course you can play the game too. The stress game. Just see if you can't. And the first thing to check is your heart beat. A little fast maybe? Yes? And your breathing – similar? And then there's the dry mouth and increasingly sweaty palms? We're looking here at Stage One of stress, and it's no mean achievement.

But you may be more ambitious than that. You may

in fact be an intermediate candidate, in which case, alongside the previous symptoms, you should also be boasting loss of creativity, and experiencing headaches, backaches or indigestion; you'll also need to be showing quite clear signs of indecisiveness, forgetfulness and some fairly muddled thinking. These are the core components of Stage Two of stress.

Advanced candidates, however, will need to be in another league altogether. Advanced candidates will need to be able to show a near-complete emotional deadness, an abyss-like loss of meaning and purpose in life and a general sense of withdrawal from friends, family and colleagues. This is the territory of Stage Three. These are the symptoms of the black belts of stress. This is burn-out. This is when, along with Apollo 13, you should be saying, 'Houston – we have a problem.' But I was never very good at saying I had a problem. No, let's rephrase that. I was *bad* at saying I had a problem. And in my eyes, Stage Three wasn't a problem. It was just the person I was. If someone cured me – God forbid! – I might just cease to exist. Anyway, it was no one else's business. So it wasn't until I got to Stage Four that I began to be worried. And Stage Four is not being able to find the ladder.

*

I'm an old man now, of course.[1] My little dance on the planet nearly done. A few more steps executed as neatly as possible, a short bow, nothing too pretentious, and that will be it. And then the Great Light. I sense it increasingly, the Great Light, one step beyond. In the meantime, though, it's a darkening late November afternoon in Caledonian Park, North London, and my feet are in the sand pit, which is big, but not quite as big as the sands of the Middle East where I spent most of my life. And all a huge mistake of course.

I was sent there to oversee the closure of the monastery of St James the Less. And let's be clear at the outset: this wasn't St Catherine's set on Mount Sinai, Mecca for pilgrims *par excellence*, featuring Moses' burning bush and a library to kill for. This was St James the Less set on the bleak edge of nowhere, never knowingly visited by Moses or indeed anyone else really. Bypassed by history, someone had finally noticed it and decided that it may be better closed down, all things being duly considered. It was just a question of choosing the right man to oversee this sharp decline. Who *was* the individual to take on this Herculean task of bringing disintegration and death to St James? Me, apparently. Yes. I was to move briskly in, and wind things up. Sixteen hundred years it had stood there, advocating its own particular sort of lunacy amid the burning noon and sun-bleached rock. And sixteen hundred years is a decent stint in anyone's book. After all, the mayfly only lives for two and a half hours. So under my gallant leadership, St James the Less was to become St James the Least and then St James the No more. Best for everyone really.

Only it didn't close. Somehow people stopped talking about closure after I arrived. I can't think why, because everything else I'd touched in life had moved swiftly in that direction. I had a good track record in this area. But what can you do? People stopped talking about closure and it seemed slightly rude to keep raising the subject. There are only so many new and exciting plans for decline that a man can propose, before he must reluctantly accept the inevitable that this organism is living and wants to continue in that vein. And so yes, I became one of those 'dropped in for a quick cup of tea and ended up staying twenty-seven years' stories, encamped amid a dry and vast infinity: a pinhead on the horizon of the world's thrusting empires.

*

Don't worry. This isn't a travelogue. I've got no sense of place at all really, though I do find this park a haunting place. Used to be a market of course – a shouting, dealing, Dickensian sort of a place, full of luvverly roses, Grimsby fish, jewellery from Bond Street and the Gin Palace for all other requirements. On a calm day you can still hear all the voices. Or so they say. But it's a calm day today and I can hear nothing but the voices which crowd my own soul. I'm a selfish man. The voice of the solicitor, for instance, telling me that an aunt I'd never met had left me a home I'd never wanted, in Islington, a place I'd never been. It wasn't that I hadn't travelled. My upbringing had been a mobile and trifle lonely affair, in the unconvincing surf of my father's business moves and my mother's low-grade depression. Australia. Singapore. The Yemen. And Crewe for nine months. It was raining as far as I remember. But no sign of Islington there.

And I hear the voice of Jacob. The solicitor had been quiet and reasoned. But when Jacob woke from his desert dream, with its vast outbreak of ladders, he was neither. 'God is here!' he'd shouted. And no one had argued. But then no one was there. The desert's like that. Not many people there. And the voice of Skarit the Rat, of course. I still heard that voice. Must have been the car backfiring in Market Road. So like gunshot, so like Skarit. Terror. Like Jacob, he'd come to call at St James the Less, but with less divine consequences.

I could tell you what happened, I suppose. Just another desert story.

Forgive me, please, but though I try and deny it, much of my heart is still there, you see. Still there in the desert. I *want* to tell you about it. I'm happy enough where I am, of course. The pensioners' club around the corner in Horace Gardens is a splendid place, and the shepherd's pie invariably hot. There's a little church nearby which seems to put up with me. It lacks imagination and a sense of communion with the saints gone by.[2] Instead, the weight and glory of our Christian inheritance is placed firmly on the shoulders of day-glo notice-boards, which for me have all the pulling power of Satan's breath. But they don't lack love at this little church and that is the main thing.

And then my newsagent's wife is the kindest woman on earth, treating me as a normal human being, notwithstanding my weekly order of the *Church Times.*[3] And yet the longing remains for the big skies and the large dry dunes. Not that the arrival of Skarit the Rat heralded a happy time for me. Exactly the opposite. But it was a time for the soul, if you know what I mean.

We could go there now. To the desert. To St James the Less, that tired old failure of a desert monastery, which I've so inadequately described. I was the abbot, would you believe? It'll be a rambling reminiscence, the indulgence of an old man. And you won't want to listen, I know. You'll have better things to do. I can think of a few myself. And if you quietly put this down now, I'll quite understand. But for my sake, if nobody else's, I tell the story. The eager young drama teacher at Horace Gardens, with his tight black jeans and baggy top, would no doubt call it 'reminiscence therapy'. I call it vanity. And as I think I've said already, Stage Four is not being able to find the ladder ...

CHAPTER ONE

Carol's Ladder

'CONVENTIONAL wisdom sucks,' I said.

On reflection, this was a slightly un-abbotlike comment, and maybe not worthy of the trackless infinity in which we sat, but Carol, in my opinion, needed dismantling. She declared. She knew. She was sure. And she was getting on my nerves. Her brisk and breathless certainties had left me pinned to the back of my seat, in my study on the north side of the monastery. I was, of course, the heretic. And she, in her alternatively firm, loving, angry, and patronising way, was trying to save me. I wasn't on her particular path, and therefore it stood to reason that I couldn't be on any path at all. Not a half decent one anyway. After all, how could there be another path, another way of doing things, another way of believing things, other than her own? The idea was so ridiculous she'd waste no time in thinking about it. Instead, she'd give me some advice.

'No one knows anything,' I'd said.

'I beg your pardon?'

'No one knows anything. St John of the Cross.'

'Oh I was wondering when he might turn up. St John of the Cross! "He who must be quoted when in or near a desert." Yet, frankly, did anyone ever understand a word the dear man wrote?'

'"No knowledge of God which we get in this life is true knowledge." Those I think were his exact words. Not *that* complicated.'

'And not that useful either. Dribbling on about an incomplete knowledge of God – not that useful in times of crisis, Abbot. Not when people are looking for something solid, a rock in the storm of life. You obviously don't get out much. You obviously don't meet people in real need.'

I refrained from mentioning that she herself, with needs the size of the Sahara, gave the lie to that comment. Instead, I focused on the great apostle.

'I think St Paul was trying to say something similar when he said that now we see in a glass darkly – or however the modern translations have it.[4] No one knows anything, basically.'

'I would have thought that you and I at least might agree that the Church knows a few things.'

'That's certainly possible, but as a rough rule of thumb, it's best to assume not. It's best to assume that the emperor has no clothes, that the emperor is starkers in fact. Feted, cheered, enormously popular – but starkers.'

'That's hardly conventional wisdom.'

'Conventional wisdom sucks.'

'Well, really! Conventional wisdom is the Spirit of God in history.'

'Or alternatively, the same mistake made a thousand times.'

'So what *is* truth, then? Or is that a rude question?'

'It's a rude question.'

'Because you see, for those of us, unlike your good self, who *aren't* fugitives from reality; for those of us who live in the real world, and not in this large sand pit, truth matters.'

'Truth is just the story on top, isn't it? The story told by the winners, who've got their hands on the best technology, the loudest speakers, the most efficient distribution network.'

Carol paused. Not easy. And then sadly but resolutely came to her decision.

'I trust you will soon resign your orders. Resign as abbot of what I believe is still, theoretically at least, a Christian institution.'

'Resign?'

'Having lost your faith. It might be appropriate.'

'Oh, I see.'

*

Carol was widely tipped to be the first woman bishop in the Church of England – a small cold country a long way away. I'd lived there for a time and, although I'd dried out a while back in the dry desert heat, I could still occasionally feel the chill. And now was one of those occasions. Carol had been staying with us at the monastery for a few days, but this was our first serious talk. She was clearly a dynamic character. I could see how she had impressed along the way, and reached the point she had. She was a driven personality, pursuing committees on which to sit like a heat-seeking missile. She was a driven personality, but I wasn't sure she knew the driver. I did. And I didn't like him at all. The way she disposed of the crumb told me everything.

We were sharing some fruit cake she'd kindly brought. Slightly dry, but what can you do? The many crumbs on my lap made their way to the floor gradually. The one crumb on Carol's lap, when spotted, was dismissed with ruthlessness, disdain and speed. There was no egg on Carol's tie, no blot on her copy-book, no skeleton in her cupboard. And no crumb on her lap. The danger, I suppose, in people like this is that in their quest to be perfect human beings they can end up becoming inhuman beings. 'Carol must be a good girl,' Daddy said. 'Carol must be a good girl, or it's smacks. Carol *is* a good girl. Always a good girl. Carol does right. Everyone else must do right too.' Just all would have been a little easier if daddy had been a good boy too. Just all would have been much easier if daddy hadn't been an alcoholic who was always struggling to hold down his job. Makes it hard for a daddy's girl, that. Hard when daddy isn't a good boy, but you can't say. You could *never* say.

She'd come on retreat to await a letter. She'd come on retreat to await a letter from the Archbishop of Canterbury, no less. It would concern the chairing of a very key and influential working party on liturgical reform. Hardly the stuff of my dreams, but excitement and anticipation are very personal affairs. That which gets me out from between the sheets in the morning is clearly not that which knocks on Carol's bedroom door. The call, the hope, the reason – we're different. But there was also a large similarity, which I was aware of. For I too, at this time, was awaiting a letter. Oh, yes ...

You see, there was a feeling in some quarters that there were just too many desert monasteries. It had all been very well in the fifth century, of course. As you will know, inspired by Father Anthony, the whole world was rushing to the desert in the fifth century, fugitives from the rotten civilisations which ruled the planet. Then, inhuman austerities and demon-haunted vigils were very *de rigueur* among the faithful.

But demand, like the pharaohs, had died. These days, the faithful on retreat tended to be less concerned about the demon-haunted vigils on offer and more concerned about tea-making facilities at the end of their corridor. A different sort of vision, and one the desert had struggled to cope with. Hence the 'feeling in some quarters', that St James the Less should go. A new word, previously unheard of in the deserts of the world, was making its entrance: rationalisation.

The word rationalisation is not a desert word, of course. Simplicity, Purity, Struggle. These are desert words. But not rationalisation. What's the point of the desert if it's rational? How could it have imprinted eternity on the mind and heart of western civilisation if it had set out to be rational? Its sheer half-starved and scurvy-ridden lunacy was the whole point. The medium was the message, and the message was: Look! Weep! Live! But apparently, there was 'a feeling in some quarters' that things all needed to get a little more reasonable now. That our neighbour, the Monastery of the Sacred Heart, should undergo a complete overhaul (or a 'heart bypass' as the contractor called it), including tea-making facilities at the end of every corridor; and that maybe, just maybe, the monastery of St James the Less had reached the end of its natural life.

I had in fact originally come to close it down. This was true. But that was over twenty years ago. Since then, it had become my home. All very unprofessional. But there we are. Now however, the feeling in some quarters was that rationalisation *could* be a desert word, that tea-making facilities *should* grace the Sacred Heart, and that St James the Less *may* need to be closed in the greater scheme of things. Yes, I too was awaiting a letter. And the waiting finds you out, doesn't it?

She was still there. Carol. Which is probably more than I would have been. Like with the early pages of a book, a first and difficult encounter with another human being presents a very big temptation to jump ship, take my leave. What, after all, is in it for me? I don't know the person. I don't want to know the person. I know enough people. I know too many in fact. There is nought to hold me here. No webs of relationship, no bonds of trust, no history of shared experience, no mutual attraction, no anticipation of glory, and sometimes, not even any coffee. I shall leave. I shall go. But as I say, Carol hadn't.

'I trust you will soon resign your orders. Resign as abbot of what I believe is still, theoretically at least, a Christian institution.'

'Resign?'

'Having lost your faith – it might be appropriate.'

'Oh, I see.'

'Well?'

'Don't imagine that I haven't considered it, Carol. And I think I will. Yes.'

'Good.'

'In fact, I'm sure I will.'

'I'm very glad to hear it.'

'Yes, when I finally cease to fire the sharp dart of longing love at the dark clouds of unknowing, I will resign; when the cross of Christ no longer holds together the fractured soul of the world, I'll definitely call it a day; and when the story of the resurrection no longer resonates hope down the empty corridors of the universe the towel will be thrown in very quickly believe me –'

'Yes, all right, all right.'

'– and when the God who is a community of love no longer welcomes me in precious friendship. When I've finally seen through all that, as I've seen through so much else, as I see through you, then yes, I'll resign. *Then* I'll leave the last chance saloon. There wouldn't be a lot to hang around for, would there? No. But until that time –'

Pause.

'So that's "the story on top" for you, is it?' asked Carol pointedly.

'Yes. Best story in the world. It's really *very* good.'

'I see,' said Carol, sounding very much like a teacher who had tried to checkmate a pupil, failed, and was now playing for time.'

'No you don't. You don't see very far beyond the end of your nose, Carol. But that's quite all right. I neither expect that you see or demand it.'

There was a silence. It wasn't a long one. It wasn't as long as one of Jane Austen's sentences, for instance. But then they're very long indeed. Apart from the Great Wall of China, they're the only human constructions visible from the moon. But it was a silence nonetheless.

And during it, I tried to look at Carol with as kindly eyes as I could muster.

'I'd prefer it if you didn't look at me as though I were an idiot,' she said.

'Don't worry. I look at myself in the same way. I am Peter the Fool after all. And you, Carol. What will be your name?'

*

One of the traditions of St James was the adoption, by both permanent and temporary members of the community, of a name; a name which said something core, something central about the inner compulsions which drove them. So I was Peter the Fool, for instance, because I had this thing about being wise. I wanted to understand the world before breakfast. It was largely a survival mechanism left over from my childhood, overstaying its welcome. Then it had protected me. Understand everything and everyone and no one's going to catch me out. So I would observe and I would understand. I would understand and I would survive. And very right and proper too. Survival is not unimportant. But there is a thin line between what the therapists call survival techniques and the old testament prophets call idolatry. And it was a line I'd frequently crossed in my adult life.

For wisdom isn't God. Understanding isn't God. It's a bit-part character, not the head honcho, and so I really shouldn't be saluting it with quite such vigour and zest every time I pass it in the corridor. It is time to grow up. I will never *leave* my childish ways. They are too much part of me. But I can at least *recognise* them as such. So let me be Peter the Fool. Let my name refer me to a central absurdity in my life which I find it rather hard to escape from; a central absurdity which actually holds me back from good things like trust, community and involvement; a central absurdity which I sometimes treat as God.

Everyone must choose their own name, of course. No one can choose one for you. No one can say, 'You will be called this' or 'You will be called that.' It is a personal discovery and a personal decision. But not one to be rushed into. We must remember that not only do we not know ourselves. But we do not know that we do not know ourselves. So first, we must learn the skill of listening to our lives. It's a painful apprenticeship, as any worthwhile apprenticeship must be. You don't suddenly become a great cabinet-maker overnight. You don't suddenly become self-aware overnight. But at the end, we come out of this apprenticeship with a trade – and maybe it's the most practical trade of all, more practical even than plumbing or camel-combing. The trade is self-awareness: an inner awakening, an appreciation of the voices various which nag us within. We recognise them now. We know their origins. Why they're there, and why they say what they say. We still salute them when they speak, of course. Old habits die hard. But we do it with less vigour than before, less zest. There isn't the old crispness and whip in the arm and hand movements. For increasingly, we are becoming able to discern between *their* persuasive tones and the still small voice of God. They are not the same, you see, not remotely, though it's the very devil to distinguish between them sometimes ...

Which is why at St James we enjoy the adoption of accurate names – lest anyone ever imagine that they are strong; which is why we at St James hugely appreciate the grace of God, which always holds our warted absurdities in such a forgiving and gentle place; and which is also why the desert makes people so downright angry sometimes. There is no assent in the desert for their blindspots, lies, vanities and deceits. Rather, on offer in the desert is an apprenticeship; a glorious ascent to nought ...

*

There was a knock on the door. It was Ted the Yes. Ted

the building contractor who was with us for a few days to oversee, among other things, some remedial work on our roofing and stone fascias. Ted the building contractor who had to say yes, even when the answer was no or maybe. Ted had no pretensions about being a member of the community of faith. But had gladly adopted some of our odd customs. The adoption of a name for himself was one of them. With penetrating insight, Ted went straight for 'the Yes'. Above telling the truth, Ted had to please. So, without hesitation or remorse, he would lie. Thus if he knew I wanted the generator serviced before Sunday, it definitely would be. Definitely. The fact that three weeks on, the generator remained limpingly unserviced made no difference. It was still 'definite' as far as Ted was concerned. No problem. No problem at all. No problemero, guv'nor. He'd speak to the man today. Sort it. He's on another job at the moment, but he'll be around this afternoon. Definitely. Ted the Yes.

'I found the ladder you were asking for, guv'nor.'

'Thank you, Ted. You're an angel in our midst. And it's all right to leave it in the chapel?'

'No problem. I'll do it myself.'

'I'll need it there for evening prayers tonight. Seven p.m. That won't be a problem?'

'Like I said, it's as good as done.'

'Good.'

'So what's it for then?'

'Ever heard of Jacob's ladder?'

'Can't say I have, guv. Is it that new flip-back sort, with the aluminium extensions?'

'Er, no. Jacob was an old rogue who had a dream. About a ladder. A few thousand years ago now.'

'Must have been a good one then. I forget mine before I even get the kettle on.'

'It was a good one, yes. It was a very good one. Made a big impression on him, anyway. He bedded down in the desert, with a stone for a pillow, and experienced a cracker – saw heaven and earth linked by a ladder, and angels moving up and down. The invasion of earth by heaven. I believe that, you see. Being a mad old abbot, I believe the invasion goes on. I believe heaven is here, so it's always been a favourite story of mine. And it's our theme over the next few days. Thought a "live" ladder in the chapel might help.'

'No problem. It'll be there. I'll sort it. Mind you, it's covered in crap at the moment, if you'll pardon my French. I'll tell Ricky to clean it.'

'Keep the crap, Ted. That's better in a way. More honest. Most accurate.'

*

'The ascent to nought?' queried Carol.[5]

'The ascent to nought. It's a great journey.'

Carol, however, clearly didn't agree. Carol was frankly incredulous. Incredulous. She made no bones about her ambition, spoke quite freely about it. Ambition was a good thing, a godly thing. There was nothing to be gained hiding lights under bushels. There's no care without power. There's no reform without power. She wanted to care. She wanted reform. She wanted power. The reason she was quite so interested in chairing this liturgical working party was that it would be such an obvious stepping stone to a bishopric – when such things were possible for a woman in the little cold country that was England. Hence her interest in the letter which would soon be carried across the desert sea. I'm told that in the movie, the postman always knocks twice. At St James, given the distance from the gate to the main building, the irregular hours of the door-keeper, and the broken bell, the postman generally knocks about fifty times, then swears a lot, and then resorts to frustrated kicks at the old gate house door.

*

That night we did indeed consider Jacob[6] in our evening prayers, set amid the deep candle-calm of our tomblike monastery chapel. The ladder, of course, wasn't there. That was also definite. But then why had I dared imagine otherwise? I tried to weave its non-appearance into my reflections. Something about all of us waiting for the ladder of God's invasion; how for many who walk the desert path, there is the strong sense of this being the last chance saloon; of having been worn down by the waiting, and crying out for heaven to be opened now. Yes, we need the ladder *now*. But, as tonight, the ladder doesn't always come to order, despite the promise, despite the 'definitely'. One or two were able to smile in recognition. One or two were too angry to smile. The last chance saloon is not always a desperately humorous or happy place to sit.

Not that Jacob felt himself to be in the last chance saloon. Far from it. He was just a rogue, pulling another scam; another conman with an eye for the main chance, prepared to deceive brother and father in pursuit of it, and now legging it unceremoniously out of town. Or out of tent, at least. Having done his best to destroy his family, he was moving on. And it was in such unpromising spiritual circumstances that God decided to give Jacob the red-carpet treatment; it was in such circumstances that God opened the heavens for Jacob, giving him a glimpse of something he couldn't easily forget. Quite simply, through dream, he sang Jacob a new song – a song he hadn't been sung in his cradle. As Ted had pointed out, not many dreams last three thousand years. Not many dreams last beyond the early morning kettle ...

And Carol's dreams? She'd spoken them clear enough. Tonight though, she sat impassive. She didn't give much away. Too professional. She didn't want to give herself a name. Thought it was all too silly for words. Her name was Carol Lock and that was that. I could imagine her sitting there stewing inwardly at God's too-gracious-by-far treatment of the Jacob who was not a do-right person at all in Carol's book. She was more of a just-desserts person. And I wondered what the ladder would look like for her. Yes, she was successful. But she needed a ladder, a ladder to release the coming and going of the angels a little more freely in her life. We'd see. Most of life is waiting of course. It's what we do in the meantime which is important. Traditionally, of course, the meantime was meant for love. Fine. But first, I had a little hate to squeeze in.

CHAPTER TWO

Tear-Sing's Ladder

I'D always found it difficult to love the monastery of the Sacred Heart and Abounding Mercy, to give it its full name. I'd also always found it difficult to love their smooth and cash-attracting Abbot Donaldo. But I was worse now. Now I was considering declaring war on them.

The monastery of the Sacred Heart was our nearest neighbour, fifty miles or so to the east. Built on the great Mount Shameon, it looked down on the plain of Mackish. It also looked down on us. No, I had always found it difficult to love. But as I say, I was now considering declaring war. As if the pendulum of life hadn't swung enough in their favour already, they now wanted us to house Constantino the Boy for the foreseeable future, during their 'redevelopment'. They'd never wanted him in the first place, as far as I could tell. Now, under the cover of major surgery, they were seizing the moment, and doing a little deft off-loading. Care in someone *else's* community. Always a good idea.

But frankly, I had enough on my plate already. It was a time of change in the community of St James. It was therefore also a time of insecurity in the community. And when a community is insecure, then the leader really earns his or her money. Ask Moses. And if he's out, I'm prepared to fill you in myself. Alongside the rumours of possible closure, which really do no one apart from stress counsellors any good at all, it was also a time of arrivals and departures. A significant departure had been our door-keeper Cassian, who'd left us suddenly to follow his life's passion and work for the very worthy Homes for Ageing Camels organisation in Cairo. (Those ageing camels with a mind to end it all could do worse than try crossing the road there.) Cassian was yet to be replaced and, although a community can exist happily for a long time without an abbot, a door-keeper is missed after about five minutes.

Meanwhile, I had two new members of the community. There was the young and energetic Sister Bernadette who struggled with her English (or her 'Ingylish') but not with her sense of mission: if it moved, organise it. If it didn't, file it. Our other new arrival was Dalip – so earnestly trying to care for me that his mere presence in the room left me drained of all life. He clearly liked to 'get alongside' people, which is all well and good, as long as you're sure those you are 'getting alongside' want to be boarded. I didn't, of course. I hadn't come to the desert for the counsellor's all-absorbing understanding and the quiet but aimless drift into the bottomless pit of emotions with questions like, 'You've said how you feel. But how do you *really* feel?' No. I had come to the desert for accuracy, simplicity, eternity, and maybe one day, love. In the meantime, I was hiding from young Dalip, who had merely become another threat. 'Friendly fire' is the technical term, I think. And really, life is quite hostile enough, without those who are theoretically supporting me threatening my life.

Dalip was from India. But with only six hundred million to care for there he clearly felt constricted. I was going to mention it quietly to Sanjay. Sanjay the Mouse. For he was from that part of the world too. Sri Lanka, I believe. Perhaps he could be an intermediary. But then he was so cautious and quiet an individual that he was really very close to disappearing altogether, and the idea of him putting his head above the parapet in the difficult business of peacemaking, faintly ridiculous. There was also the fact that, for some reason, Dalip *never* spoke with him, never got alongside him. Sanjay the Mouse. Jokes from the 'unable to fight his way out of a paper bag' or 'so angry I could crush a grape' stable were not unknown in the cloisters. So he was probably not the person to seize Dalip by the throat and bid him call off the dogs of concern.

Mind you, I'll say this for Sanjay: he was continuity and he was stability. He'd been with us six years or so, and he wasn't leaving, and he wasn't in the middle of huge emotional turmoil. So amid the changes and chances of monastery life at the moment, he was a stable figure of sorts. Silent, but stable. Invisible, but stable. And for that I was duly grateful. Not ecstatic. But duly grateful.

*

Now however the Monastery of the Sacred Heart and Abounding Mercy wanted us to have Constantino the Boy. For this, I wasn't duly grateful. Nor was I unfeignedly thankful. It wasn't his age which was the problem. Constantino was eighty-seven, relatively young for the desert. No. The problem was that Contantino had Alzheimer's. Senile dementia. Call it what you like, but carers know the cost. It's not a glamorous calling for anyone. Life is a terrible brevity, but it's a brevity which can take a very long time.

I couldn't say no, of course. If I said no, Constantino would inevitably turn out to be an angel in disguise, which would all be very embarrassing. Too much of a chance to take. And so yes, of course Constantino could come and stay with us, he'd be most welcome, when would be the most convenient time for him to arrive? With almost indecent haste he was being sent tomorrow afternoon. Tomorrow afternoon? It was a development in the back of my mind as I sat three hours after sunrise, with Tear-Sing the Sad.

*

His life, in brief, was Chinese orphanage, Tianamen Square, Parisian Design Centre, New York fashion house, St James the Less. By trade, he designed jewellery to adorn beautiful clothes. He would sit alone surveying the New York skyline, suck breath fresheners, sigh, adjust his colourful little waistcoat with his long precise fingers, and then dream and draw the exquisite. Downstairs, technicians skilled in metal and stone waited – waited to take his dreams, weld his exquisites, and make them flesh. It all sounded very perky if you liked that sort of thing. And he did. But. There's always a 'but'. Why does the soul always insist on a 'but' when it could be out there enjoying itself. But then, perhaps that's what makes it a soul …

Tear-Sing sat with me, sipped tea, nibbled a dry desert biscuit, cleverly seeking out crumbs with his tongue before they fell, and talked of funerals remembered, autumns experienced and suicides contemplated. Tears came easily to his eyes, but they could never fill the abyss of sadness along who's edge he walked. Little, lost and lonely – beautifully tragic, tragically beautiful, and at this very moment, very, very angry that the community was not delivering what he desired.

'They are not there for me,' said Tear-Sing in the, I suppose predictable, but indescribable, Chinese/French/American mix.

'No,' I said, knowing that argument at this stage was quite useless, and would merely confirm me as another part of the problem. That would come soon enough anyway. Beware the projections, abbot's rule number one.

'Bernadette, she harasses me. She tells me I should be "tugging at my stockings" many times. I don't know what she's talking about. She's mad or something. She's a, how-you-say, harridan?'

'My guess is that she's telling you to pull your socks up. She's still coming to grips with the finer points of colloquial English, but eager in the meantime.'

'I find that completely unacceptable.'

'Yes.'

'I don't find that helpful.'

'No.'

'Really I don't. She understands nothing of me. Nothing.'

'Dalip?'

'He is young. He could not bear the weight of all I must speak. Is it unreasonable that I should demand at least to be understood? Is it unreasonable to hope that my loneliness will be understood?'

*

I didn't often feel lonely. I may have appeared a lonely figure to some but I didn't feel lonely. In fact, to my knowledge, I'd only felt lonely twice in my life. Once, at Christmas time, when I'd stood by a childhood fire in a room that was empty. There was no one around. With the best will in the world, everyone was somewhere else that Christmas, around other people, around other fires. Alone by the fire on Christmas day. I'd felt lonely then. And I'd felt longing. And I'd felt sad. And I'd felt small.

Fifteen years later, as a member of a religious community, I'd stormed out quietly into the night when there was no one there for what I needed and wanted at that time. No sadness this time. Just anger. Stamping-my-little-feet fury. I'd hold my breath. I'd hold it until I turned blue. And *then* what would mummy do? *Then*, she'd have to come and find me. *Then* she'd have to pay. Fancy letting *me* down like that!

But now, loneliness wasn't big on my horizon. In fact, loneliness wasn't really on my horizon at all. My scars had hardened and hidden the wound below. I couldn't rustle up the 24-carat self-pity so effortlessly managed by Tear-Sing. Indeed, larger on my horizon was the opposite. Happy in my castle with the draw-bridge up, my dread was the sight of people approaching. With luck, they'd go away. With less luck, they may require from me a brief chat from the parapets. With no luck at all, they'd ask to come in. They'd ask me to lower the drawbridge, open the gate and invite them in. Oh dear. Fear. Bad day. And when would they be leaving? I'd need to know that. I didn't fear Satan. But I did fear people who dropped in on the off-chance.

I had a dream, though. And in my dream it was different. In my dream I would invite people in. Not a castle but a home. And I would say welcome and I would say this is my home and I'd like to show you round. And I would relax. And I would laugh. And I wouldn't mind what people saw. And I'd talk about the rooms, telling what each meant to me. And they could open cupboards and poke around dark corners, and if they found things they could hold them up and say, What's this? without me asking them exactly what business it was of theirs. This is my home. Enjoy.

Just a dream, of course. Only a dream. But was it also an invasion of sorts? A divine and gentle invasion into my cramped and so-called life?

*

'Is it unreasonable to hope that my loneliness will be understood?' Tear-Sing asked again.

'Very probably,' I said, and continued with my jigsaw. It was a small failing of mine which most people kindly allowed. Strangely, it helped me to listen, and enabled me to forget about all that ridiculous body language business, which the Sacred Heart did summer courses on. Thus, Sydney Opera House was taking shape nicely before my eyes, though the large expanse of Sydney sky was a bit of a worry. A brilliant blue sky undisturbed by variation. A storm cloud would have helped greatly. Tear-Sing obliged.

'I thought *you* might understand.'

'Me? Understand? Why on earth would you imagine that?'

'You are the abbot.'

'Ye-es,' I said hesitantly in the way one might agree with someone who, out of the blue, had just said that tomatoes are red. It's not that you're disagreeing. Its just that you're wondering what it has to do with anything.

'I've heard you speak. I sensed in your words that you might. Might understand.'

'That's a heavy burden to lay on someone.'

'To expect them to understand? A heavy burden? I would have called it a basic requirement.'

'No. There's nothing basic about that. Just impossibility. And danger. For just suppose I understood you a little, one day I won't. One day I will misunderstand you. Sooner rather than later I will misunderstand you. I, who would understand the entire universe before breakfast, believe me, will misunderstand you. I'll misunderstand you three times before the cock crows. Then how will you feel?'

Tear-Sing paused, breathed in deep, his head staring down into his lap. These were difficult things. He prodded at the crumbs on his plate. He adjusted his position in the chair, glanced at me, looked down again, and then away into the beyond, which is a bit of a feature of the desert. It's very strong on the beyond.

'I will feel very betrayed,' he said. 'I will feel very

angry. I feel that now. I feel let down by this community. By you. Very let down by you. Let down at the time I most needed people to be there for me.'

'I think it was the Buddha. Yes, almost certain. Said that community life was like sword grass in one's hand. Something to be endured. *But*, God help the soul which removes itself from that enduring.'

A pause. And then for accuracy's sake, I added, 'That second bit was mine. The bit about the soul removing itself from that enduring. That wasn't the Buddha. Wouldn't want him turning in his nirvana at being misquoted.'

'I do not find that helpful to me at the moment.'

'No.'

'I cannot take my place in this community. Not at the moment. It is too painful. Much too painful.'

'Yes.'

We sat in silence for a while. I contemplated the Opera House again. I hadn't realised how similar the various roof cones actually were. It wasn't just the sky that was causing problems. And then, of course, there was Tear-Sing as well.

'One day,' I added, 'it might actually be different. Hard to imagine, I know, but one day you may be able to say in your heart, "I alone and God are in this world," and *then*, I think, you may find peace. When you can handle the alone, without the self-pity and without the anger, *then* I think, you might also find community, strangely enough. When the leaning on others is over, the loving can begin. But then, who am I to say? It's a tall order certainly. And I am Peter the Fool.'

There were tears in Tear-Sing's eyes. Wet-eyed frustration, moist-eyed longing – here was a well which could water the very desert itself. He continued to play with the crumbs on his plate, pushing, shaping, forcing, using the dampness on his fingers to mould and gel. And almost unthinkingly, with the apparent effortless ease of the genius, he created there amid the humdrum of leftovers, a cross which wept. A crying cross of biscuit bits, set on a cracked china plate. Such beauty, such pain, such anger. I prayed that Tear-Sing the Sad would find his ladder. Not through me, of course – but despite me …

*

That night we sat in the chapel where the saints had sat for sixteen hundred years. And every day for sixteen hundred years the divine liturgy celebrated, the prayers spoken. Sometimes I leant heavily on them.[7] The sheer 'carriedness' of us all by those who had gone before.

The sheer partnership of existence with those who had gone before. A regular communion of toss-pots and lunatics like myself who had now handed the baton to me. And they would help me towards holiness. They would save me from the spiritual amnesia which knows only the present, reinvents the wheel weekly, and sails full steam ahead towards the nearest dominant novelty and euphoria.

No, it is a restless and exhausting business living only from the present. Wretched. The chapel was saving me from it. Cut into the huge rock which rose above the monastery on the east side, it was a place heavy with prayer, groaning with history and dripping with wax. Still no ladder, though. Ted had assured me that it would be with us tonight. He couldn't foresee any problems on that score. You will have your ladder, Father Peter! Yesterday, difficulties, but tonight, it really was definite. Only it wasn't.

But there *was* a ladder in Jacob's dream. Oh yes. Opening heaven to earth and earth to heaven, as God reached out for Jacob in the dark speech of the Spirit. God could have sent a stern desert prophet to Jacob. Stern dress. Stern eating habits, involving the luxury of locusts only on high days and holidays. And the stern desert prophet could have said stern desert things to this wastrel. Sternly. Instead, Jacob is given a dream. Instead, Jacob receives a dream, and not any old dream, but a dream from the very top drawer. And into his imagination and will explodes the ladder of possibility. Things will never quite be the same again. And he is terrified, of course – terrified by this turbulent invasion of his lethal life. In between the terror, there were low-lying outbreaks of ecstasy and thrill. But mainly, it was terror. Who was this God exactly?

The following day, for us as a community, it was a different sort of invasion. No low-lying ecstasy for us. No thrill. Just terror. Exclusive one hundred per cent proof terror ...

CHAPTER THREE

Snakes and Ladders (without the Ladders)

WHEN exactly did the last boat on the river out of Eden leave? It's really very hard to be sure. All desert dwellers know that it has, however. They know that it has left. But now the creeping feeling that it wasn't just leaving. It was disintegrating. The impression that ours was now not just a wistful cruise from Eden towards a vaguely uncertain future. But that ours was a vessel broken-backed and helpless in the midst of tidal crash and surge. We'd run aground on a terrible vengeance, and Tear-Sing was screaming, floored and face-down in the courtyard dust, bloody mouthed, a soldier-fist pressed hard to his spine. The commander held high above his head the small bird.

'Lesson one!' he shouted, strutting and breathless, 'Lesson one!'

This was sneer and assault; the bullying hectoring verbal hammer of the barrack hut, as we waited. The community of St James the Less stood huddled against the west wall, cornered and captive. Young, harsh male arrogance, dressed to kill, swarmed the place, rounding up, harassing, pushing, frenetic and rude. Sanjay the Mouse was the last to appear, frog-marched to where the rest of us stood. And in the midst of it all, the sick circus barker, the commander.

'Lesson one! Everyone's a winner! Everyone's a winner if they obey. But if they don't –'

Set before us was a large covered box. The commander approached it, paused next to it.

'If they don't –'

The covering was pulled off. Beneath it, a large metal cage. Inside the cage, scuttling and thrusting, a huge rat.

'My best friend!' shouted the commander.

'Not overburdened with rivals,' whispered Carol in my ear.

'Everyone's a winner till they disobey me! Then they are not winners. This bird is not a winner!'

The bird was Tear-Sing's. A desert thrush, lame-winged and adopted in its tragedy by one who understood. It had been snatched from his hands by the commander. Tear-Sing lay quiet. He still watched. But quiet. He knew. We all knew.

'When people disobey, they are not winners. They are losers. They are losers like this bird is a loser. And what happens to losers?'

'Oh, for God's sake,' muttered Carol.

'*This is what happens to losers!*'

The cage opened on top. The bird was thrown in. It was destroyed instantly in a squeak and a fluff of red-wet feather.

'My name is Skarit! You will fear that name! You will fear *me*! And you – *you* – will come out here!'

He was gesturing to someone or something which had caught his attention. Up till now, we'd been watching something prepared, something predictable. This was different. This was unrehearsed and dangerous. Skarit seemed threatened. Before, we'd all known what would happen but we didn't know now.

'You will come here! Yes, you! *You!*'

We followed his eyes to Sanjay, who was being dragged forward. Mistaken identity surely? He was stood before us, neither tall nor short but almost lifeless next to the animation of Skarit. Skarit waved away the guards. They were alone together. With the rat.

Skarit was back in studied control, confident with the setting, familiar with the arena and sure of the outcome.

'Lesson one! Everyone's a winner if they obey! But if they disobey ... *You!*'

He walked round Sanjay. Circling. Circling the Mouse. Sanjay stood very still. In all the years I'd known him, I'd never really looked at him. He wasn't that sort of person. I could imagine him as a slightly down-at-heel solicitor in Calcutta – or the teacher who'd been in the school for twenty years and still no one quite knew where he lived or what he did at weekends. At this very moment, though, he wasn't doing anything. The only visible movement in him was in his eyes. They were watching. And Skarit was circling.

'You will show us what you did.'

Sanjay said nothing. And trusted no one. Not really. He'd come to the desert seeking to learn trust; seeking to get beyond the fear that the relationship may end, so much better all round not to trust it in the first place. Better to hold back. Always hold back. Give nothing and they won't be able to take it away. Like his mother, for instance. His father had died not long after he was born. Around long enough to provide a little brother for Sanjay, though. For four years he and his brother had had the undivided attention of his mother. But then as his fifth birthday approached, his mother had married again. First, he gained an unwanted step-father. Then he lost a wanted mother, as she moved out with her new partner and a maternal grandmother moved in to look after him. He lost his younger brother too. They felt he was just too young to be left. How thoughtful.

So Sanjay liked the weather-beaten walls of the monastery of St James. You could trust them. They weren't going anywhere. And he liked animals – indeed his cell was something of an animal hospital – because they were altogether simpler than people, and you generally knew where you stood with them. As regards humans, there was a gentle paranoia in him, of course, but hostility towards them was very under control and his relationships were nearly always polite, if rather rigid and formalised in manner. Paralysingly shy, paralysingly submissive, hence 'the Mouse'. And at this particular moment, the Mouse was very exposed. A long way from a safe hole in the wall, with all paths of escape seemingly blocked …

'*You will show us what you did! With your hands!* You will show us what you did with your hands when the bird died. You did something. I didn't like it. I want you to show everyone. So everyone can see what I don't like.'

The sweat was trickling into Sanjay's eyes, amid the ranting. Thus far, though, his hands had remained by his side. Now movement. Slowly, he began to raise his right arm. We joined with him in weighing the consequences. Every decision a crisis. Time slowed. I was watching the watchers of this drama. Some hands were reaching out to others' hands. Carol seethed in strong aloneness. Here was the character Skarit *should* have been taking on. Not Sanjay. Not Sanjay the Mouse.

'Do it!' shouted Skarit.

And then Sanjay did. He did it. And said it.

'In the name of the Father, and in the name of the Son and in the name of the Holy Spirit ...'

And with these words he falteringly signed the sign of the cross, from head to abdomen, from left shoulder to right shoulder, but it reached beyond, allowing each of us to feel again the strong touch of the one who'd opened wide his arms for us on the cross. Skarit sensed the shift in power. He reached for his gun.

'Not again! Never again! Is that understood? No one will ever do that again! Do you understand!'

We understood. It had been a brief revolution of the Spirit. But we understood now. Apart from Sanjay. Because then Sanjay went and spoiled everything. I can still hear him now, across the courtyard, across the years, across eternity.

'In the name of the Father, and the Son and the Holy Spirit – we *live*! Amen.'

We were stunned by Sanjay's confident words. Stunned by the confident cross which he drew again from forehead to abdomen, from left shoulder to right. Stunned by his defiance, his rebellion. So stunned in fact that we all forgot ourselves and joined in the 'Amen'.

*

That afternoon, Constantino the Boy arrived, in all his disturbing madness. By the time he did, a gallows was already under construction in the courtyard. I was an hour away from a meeting with Skarit, to plead for the life of Sanjay. And it hadn't slipped my mind that I was due to reflect that night on Jacob's post-dream exclamation, 'God is here!' So just another day, really . . .

The car was impounded, of course, and the driver joined the rest of the community under house arrest in the chapel. Unfortunately, Skarit insisted that Constantino must also go there. Not, however, till I'd shown this irritating little man who repeated himself the whole time around his new home.

'I'm eighty-seven,' he said. 'Eighty-seven years old, I am.'

'Well, the mayfly only lives for two and a half hours, so you're doing well.'

No effective treatment for Alzeimer's, of course. A certain sense of therapeutic nihilism, in fact, in the ranks of the professional carers. Nothing works. So in the meantime, we'll bung in some reminiscence therapy, a little reality orientation, a smattering of music therapy, some personal biography and generally seek to maximise the spared abilities. What does not appear on that list is 'enforced captivity with a bunch of desert no-marks in cave'. This was going to look great in the *International Journal of Psychiatry*.

We went together to the kitchens and the refectory.

'Here is where the food is made.'

'Very nice. I'm eighty-seven, you know.'

'Yes, you mentioned.'

There's a terrible despair in loss of memory. For once it's gone, that which is becomes the only way. As I said, there's no holiness in amnesia, spiritual or otherwise. The grip of the present is total. For only memory can give a sense of possibility, a sense of future, a way ahead.

'My father. He'll be collecting me. I must be going now.'

'If you could just stay a while.'

'All right then. But he'll be collecting me. He always does. I'm eighty-seven.'

'Yes, you are. Quite young for eternity really.'

Constantino had been a bit of a legend in the desert. He had been a master chef in Italy, well known for his culinary flair and daring; and well known too for a social diary he never had, but which was always full. He was the boy who'd never quite grown up. Attention-span brief, energy endless. He'd then served in the desert during World War Two, and never left. As he himself had written, it had apparently exposed in him 'a windy emptiness, a great flitting hither and thither, leaving me raw and unskilled in even the lightest practice of solitude. I felt many-winged follies of my soul. But contrition came hard. I worked the desert kitchens. I like to think I introduced pasta to the camels! But I worked also with the raisins, the pomegranates, the couscous and the eggs. You can be surprising even with those! And then to the hermit holes set in the deserts of Calamus and Porphyrio – vaster stretches than even the desert of Scete. It was a walk of seven or eight days to penetrate those wastes. And there I found a deeper contrition. There, maybe, the Boy grew up a little ...'

The legend. Now the fag-end, who nobody quite

knew what to do with. We were the nearest the ashtray …

*

The left arm of Stalin was badly warped. It was askew at the elbow, leading to a deformity in his left hand, which he was unable to use freely. It wouldn't open properly. But then untreated fractures of the left arm are frequent in battered children. Obvious really. It's the area of their body most vulnerable to right-handed assault. To ask mercy from Stalin, therefore, didn't tend to be a very profitable exercise. Stalin had asked it from *his* father and failed, and really, what you've never received yourself is hard to pass on to others.[8] So it was 'Go straight to the Gulag. Or to bullet in the head. Do not pass Go. And don't even think about collecting £200.'

I had the nagging feeling that a similar reception awaited me, as I sat down with the belligerent, pot-bellied anti-social thug called Skarit, who had a gut full of aggression and a head full of cunning, but no heart to mediate between the two. I suspected that history would record that it hadn't been a very profitable exercise pleading for the life of Sanjay.

'You are, of course, most welcome here,' I said. 'You and your men. Hospitality to the traveller is a tradition we cherish, whatever it is which brings the traveller to our door.'

I'd lost my desk. Skarit sat there in my place. He seemed to like that. I was very afraid for the Sydney Opera House, which lay vulnerable before him, but fortunately, he seemed to like that too, adding at least three pieces of sky while we talked. I wasn't so thrilled about the gun emplacement in my window, though. I think we were talking effect rather than necessity. The war which had soiled the desert skies was over. What precisely this unit was doing here I wasn't sure. It all had the feel of posturing. The words 'largely' and 'unnecessary' hung heavy in the air.

But then my guess was that very few things Skarit did in his life were necessary, beyond the confines of his own cramped and damaged perception. His golden rule was that you should do unto others before they do unto you. Hit hard and hit low. Stay alert and stay on top. When the world is perceived as a battlefield, an arena of survival, such are the necessities. Like most of the compulsions we live out of, it was devilishly and beautifully simple. Similarly, like most of the compulsions we live out of, it was completely unnecessary – a childhood toy being clung to in adulthood somewhat embarrassingly and inappropriately. In the meantime however, God help the victims which Skarit must seek out to avenge this unaltered unfeeling deep-frozen childhood rage. God help Sanjay, for instance.

'This is a picture of my mother and father,' he said proudly, showing me a black and white photo of a large man and a small, painfully thin woman. The photo was in a leather holder withdrawn from his shirt pocket, set just above where his heart should have been. 'They were fine people. Very fine people. My father was a strong man.'

*

They do say that there is only one yawn in the world, passed endlessly around. So when was the first yawn? A strong contender must surely be the first time a family photo was removed from the pocket with the words, 'You may be interested to see this.' If yawns have been dated earlier than this, it doesn't take much imagination to return to the time when the human being was a cave-dweller. It's late. The mammoth has been eaten, fire has been discovered, but the wheel is still some centuries off – so there's a slight lull in the conversation. And then the host has an idea. 'Have you seen the wall paintings of our wedding?'

But beneath my surface yawn was a much deeper

weariness in my soul. The weariness with the lie which Skarit was about to perpetrate.

'Yes, my father. He was strong. Fine and strong.'

'Your father punished you?'

'Yes! And needed to. If the child won't listen, then he must feel. That's what he would say. I was bad. I deserved it. Even the burns.'

'The burns?'

'Cigarette burns. On the arm. He knew how to punish, but, like I say, if the child won't listen, he must feel.'

'You must have felt.'

'I felt. Although the skin hardens a little after a while. But never completely.'

'Did you tell anyone?'

'Tell anyone? Who would you recommend? There was no one to tell.'

'Your mother?'

'An amazing woman, my mother. In her own way.'

'You told her?'

'No. We lived in poverty. Real poverty, you understand.'

'She didn't mind the punishments?'

'Like I said, we lived in poverty. What else could she do? She loved me though. A mother's love is a wonderful thing.'

'So you don't blame your parents?'

'Blame them? For what? I know how bad I was. I have children of my own. I know the evil in children. If they won't listen, then they must feel.'

'What must they feel?'

'Something which hurts.'

'Even burns?'

'Something which hurts. Didn't do me any harm.'

'No.'

I contemplated this fine upstanding figure of humanity, and felt exhausted. Exhausted by the clarity and certainty of the self-deception, so heavily guarded, and apparently impenetrable. I sighed. I yawned. And made one last comment.

'Nietzche calls it oblivion. Freud calls it repression. I call it lying. And I hate it whenever I see it. You're misplacing the blame. And innocent people are paying the price. People like Sanjay ...'

*

Meanwhile, back at the ranch, Ted had surpassed himself. He'd actually found a ladder. But he hadn't just found a ladder and taken it to the courtyard in double-quick time. He'd also found a good supply of wood and an old sack. This was all very good news for those constructing the gallows. Thanks were due all round to Ted the Yes. Thus the gallows was finished in record time. The ladder solved the knotty little problem of ascent onto the platform. And the sack, when filled with sand, was a marvellous dummy, a splendid stand-in for Sanjay. It meant that we could listen to the test-drops during our midday meal, prepared by Tear-Sing and watched over by four guards who when they were much older would probably need to shave.

From scraps of barbed wire used by the soldiers to create no-go areas, Tear-Sing set on each table a crown of thorns. In the midst of each crown, he'd set a candle from the chapel. If the world could be saved by beauty – tasteful, simple beauty – Tear-Sing was our saviour. He'd baked some bread. He broke it, and passed it around in silence. It was a last supper. It was a last supper for Sanjay. That was for certain. It hadn't proved a profitable exercise pleading for his life. But no one could be sure it wasn't their own last supper too. Skarit had been strutting and snarling that morning like a junkyard dog pumping high on adrenalin – aiming for the target he knew, the gut.

So whose last supper was it anyway? Mine? Certainly the pomegranates, raisins and eggs held a particular fascination. There was a vast sense of miracle and wonder about them. A case of heightened awareness, amid the communal disturbance and the sandbag jolt. And the rat. We couldn't forget the rat, because his cage had been thoughtfully placed in the refectory by Skarit, giving a sense of sharp-toothed fur-scuttling danger at the heart of that most sacred of acts: the act of eating together.

Constantino was reminding Dalip of his age. He was eighty-seven, apparently. Dalip was getting alongside him with strong eye contact. Constantino was also reminding him that very soon his father would be along to collect him, so he best be getting his coat. Carol then stepped in firmly saying that he should finish his meal first, and asking if he was enjoying it. He said he was but pointed out that he could have done it better, even with lard and camel dung as ingredients, and so Carol said that next time he should. And then Carol looked at Sanjay. I think I knew then probably, but I may be flattering myself. It wouldn't be the first time. But the eyes *are* the windows of the soul, and when Carol looked at Sanjay, I think I knew.

*

Ted left the meal early, muttering something about time

waiting for no man. Dalip got up and went over to Sanjay. Sister Bernadette was busying herself with seeing what was wrong with the meal, and nipping in and out of scullery and kitchen to sort it out. Don't worry – she'd go. Now how many spoons were needed? She could always see what was wrong. She could even see what was wrong even if everything was completely right. God may have looked at the Garden of Eden and been pleased, but Bernadette would have been able to spot the cracks. Meanwhile, Tear-Sing was wilting in this struggle for control, for the refectory was in theory his domain. Now Sanjay was holding Dalip who was crying. And then Sanjay was crying. And then Dalip was clinging and sobbing. Sanjay was holding him closer. Carol was watching them, clearly understanding the situation in a way which I wasn't. She hesitated, and then came over to see me.

'You do know that they are brothers?' she said.

I didn't.

'You mean, it was Sanjay and Dalip together at their mother's knee in those early years?'

'Yes,' replied Carol. 'And Dalip wanted to get back to that. Looks like they have in a way ...'

Had there been a camera crew at St James, the scene would have closed with a lingering shot of Sanjay and

Dalip in each other's arms. Fortunately there wasn't. Just two people struggling with the *now*, and how it *used* to be.

★

Strangely, when I think of the execution, I think of Dalip. For when the trap door opened, and Sanjay fell barefoot like a puppet on a string, Dalip broke ranks, vaulted the platform and leapt on to Sanjay, clung on him in mid-air, arms around neck, staring into his face, pulling him down, killing him and kissing him, and then falling with him to the ground. It was all over very quickly. Dalip made sure of that. We were herded back into the chapel with the promise that we could bury the body the following day. Prompt burials in the desert are important for obvious reasons. In the meantime, we were left with the scaffold words of Sanjay. 'I don't have the final answers. And it is hard to trust. But in the end, I have to act. In the end, I have to choose. In the end, I have to bet. So here's my choice. Here's my bet. In the name of the Father, and of the Son, and of the Holy Spirit. Amen!'

Sanjay the so-called Mouse.

★

God is here. Our theme at evening prayer: God is here. The terrified and awe-filled Jacob wakes from his dream proclaiming God's strange presence in this place. Truly, God abides in this site and I was not aware! We nodded in recognition. We understood. Jacob had had a dream. We'd had a nightmare. But we understood. Same conclusion. It was just that ours was a quieter conclusion. Silent even. It wasn't an excited exclamation. Just a wordless but steel-strong awareness. God is here. Interestingly though, Ted the Yes wasn't. Judas had stepped out into the night ...

CHAPTER FOUR

The Place of the Graves

'I will be Skarit the Rat,' said Skarit. 'You like your little name games here, don't you? I will join in. I will be Skarit the Rat.'

'We like accuracy,' I said.

'That *is* accurate,' said Carol.

We were walking, dressed for the desert, covered from head to toe in long loose clothing, protecting us from frying sun and stinging sand and dust, whipped and tossed by the rising wind. We were walking to the Place of the Graves to bury Sanjay. Skarit, Carol and myself had briefly become an unlikely item on this unlikely pilgrimage.

'Fear. Have you seen the fear the rat provokes? Have you seen the way it breaks the human spirit? I like that.

I like that very much indeed. It is a wonderful quality. Priceless.'

Skarit's small talk was nothing if not unusual.

'You're not that ambitious, are you?' I said.

Skarit paused to discern the angle of attack.

'Many fear me now. One day, many more will fear me.'

'No. I meant ambitious for your soul. You're not very ambitious for your soul.'

'What are you talking about?'

'Dr George, really. Good old Dr George. Wittenberg. Germany.'

'I haven't heard of him.'

'No. Well, he's been dead four hundred and fifty years, so he's not the self-publicist he was.'

'I'm not interested in medicine. I'm interested in power.'

'Oh well, he had some of that, and wanted more. Faust was his other name. George Faust. Bit of a boy. Not a huge amount known about him. Suffice to say the rumour was that he had strange gifts. Impressed kings and bishops, which should immediately make one suspicious, of course. Then towards the end of his life he suggested that the secret of his success lay in a pact with Satan. "Give me powers on earth and in return you can have my eternal soul." Extraordinary lack of ambition on his part. To exchange tin-pot adulation for his eternal soul. While you, Skarit, are prepared to exchange yours for a little slice of short-term domination ...'

'On the contrary,' said Skarit. 'It is you desert nothings who lack ambition. You imagine an eternity which isn't there. You sell your souls to a mistaken and over-exuberant imagination.'

'Oh I see. Yes. Well, that does rather undermine my little story. If there's no eternity.'

'No eternity, no soul, Abbot. No soul, no point, Abbot. No point to your silly little religious games and your silly little religious names – Abbot. Dr George was ahead of his time.'

*

The possibility had of course crossed my mind. No, it had more than crossed my mind. In my darker moments, it had started by crossing my mind, but then once inside, had knocked down the door of my heart, and gate-crashed my gut, where it lodged as a squatter whose calling card was emptiness. The sheer undying recklessness of a belief in the beyond. Belief in a spectacular future beyond the little horizons of our three score years and ten. Of course I believed in it. And then again, of course I didn't.

It is the task of the Church on earth not only to out-love the world – but also to out-imagine it. This is not a difficult calling at present. With its disintegrating memory, separating the present from the past, the world can hardly say anything these days beyond 'I am' or 'We are.' On a very very good day, when the piper of scientific advance plays a particularly good tune, the world can wipe a tear from its eye, and say with Kafka, 'There's hope. But there's not hope for us.' But that's on a good day. And most days, as we know, are not good days. In the meantime, keep on going, can't keep on, must keep on, keep on going ...

But what if the Church's imaginings *had* all got a little exquisite? A little intoxicated? And in truth a teensy bit out of touch with reality. As abbot, I was the guardian of a never-ending story of sky-splitting proportions. But was it true, this story? It was a *good* story. But was it a true story? Or was I, in Skarit's words, just an organiser of silly religious games, gaily inviting everyone on the *Titanic* to cheer up, because if we were quick, there was time for at least one more stab at the deck quoits and maybe a hot shower afterwards. Silly religious games. And there was, of course, one of our best games coming up: the burial of Sanjay. Yes. That's why there were twelve of us walking into the middle of nowhere, following a coffin tied to the back of an army jeep, hotfoot literally to the Place of the Graves. I was thinking of staying there myself.

*

'Have you read *On the Out-Casting of Boasting?*' asked Carol.

'Not to my knowledge,' I replied.

'You surprise me. It's by a friend of yours.'

This came as a little bit of a surprise because, as far as I knew, I didn't have any friends.

'Really?' I said.

'Yes. Abbot Donaldo.'

'Ah.'

'You must know him, I presume?'

'Er, yes, I know him. Not terribly well, but I know him. Know *of* him certainly. His real name is Donald by the way. I don't know where the 'o' has come from. It's a fairly recent appendage.'

'That book of his,' continued Carol, doing a brilliant impression of someone not in the least bit interested in what I had to say, 'it's why I came to the desert. Here, I felt, was an authentically different voice.'

'So why didn't you opt for the Sacred Heart?

'I did, but it was full.'

'Oh I see.'

'Then someone said there was always space at St James the Less.'

'Well, not *always* ...'

'Mostly.'

'We had a large group of Swedish psychologists for a couple of nights last February –'

'They do say though that his recent book is even better, if that's possible. *On the Out-Casting of Pride.* A desert classic. The new Father Anthony, or so they say!'

'Who says?'

'Well, Abbot Donaldo. He was only joking of course. His self-deprecation is almost sinful. He won't have a good word said about himself. A marvellous man.'

'Quite. I'm told even God wants his autograph.'

'And what is that supposed to mean?'

Oh dear. It was meant to mean a lot of things. It was meant to mean I was groping in the dark for the ladder of eternity, and feeling only a headache coming on. It was meant to mean that, unlike Jacob, I was a long way from the heavenly invasion of the present. It was meant to mean I'd had my fill of Abbot Donaldo. It was meant to mean that each freshly sugared compliment heaped on him was salt in my tea. It was meant to mean that I'd had better days, frankly. And then things took a turn for the worse. Dalip turned up to care for me.

'I want you to know that I am here for you, Abbot Peter. In the name of Christ, I am here for you.'

'You're here for yourself, Dalip.'

'I hardly think so!'

'You hardly think.'

'I know how you feel.'

'Oh my God,' I said in a genuine sense of abandonment, as the boarding party from hell ran rampant through my psyche.

'Whatever it is you most dread – it may not happen,' he continued.

By the grace of God I managed to resist saying that it just had. But he prattled on.

'The Chinese word for crisis also means opportunity.'

I tried to be charitable. I tried to remind myself that this was friendly fire. It didn't help. It was still lethal. I tried reminding myself that this man had just lost his brother. That didn't help either. In fact it made things worse. I hated in Dalip the whole psychic tangle which demanded that he be a busybody of concern when he should be grieving, when he should be seeking a little 'alone' with his interior. So he was frightened of the emptiness within himself. So he obsessively had to reach outwards towards others to escape it. But not in the name of Christ and not in my backyard, thank you very much.

'Why did you and Sanjay never talk?'

'We had fallen out. A long time ago. I think in some ways he came here to escape me. And my family. I followed him.'

'He knew you were coming?'

'No.'

'You just turned up one day and surprised him?'

'Yes.'

'That was some invasion.'

'I had to come.'

No wonder Sanjay had been so quiet. It's called keeping your head down. But I had another bone to pick with Dalip.

'You didn't tell me either. That you were his brother. It might have been courteous, not to say honest.'

'No, I thought you might not allow it. Brothers in the same monastery. You might have asked questions. You might have talked to Sanjay about it, and who knows what he might have said. I couldn't afford to take that risk.'

'Determined *and* calculating.'

'I had to build bridges. He wasn't going to. So I had to. Otherwise, well – that was it between us and I couldn't leave it there.'

'And in a way you had to win, didn't you?'

'I don't think so. No.'

'Oh, I think you did. In a way, he'd taken you on by coming here. You, Dalip, who must have a special place in everyone's heart. You didn't appear to have a special place in his. He was taking you on. How did you feel?'

Dalip sighed. I let the silence run. And then he spoke again from a slightly more broken and questioning place within.

'I couldn't understand it.'

'No. And there's a terrible anger in rejection, isn't there?'

'Maybe. It did worry me in my early days here how restless I was. I'd come so far to help and it seemed to count for nothing.'

'And there's a terrible happiness in revenge. In winning. The Queen of Hearts. She likes to *win.* However *concerned* the winning may appear.'

'I'm not a saint, I know that.'

'In which case welcome to the desert. The chains of the unmastered past in each of us *can* begin to be dismantled – once they're acknowledged as chains and not given religious names like holiness or devotion or virtue …

We walked on in silence. It was hard not to focus on the coffin ahead, kindly knocked up by Ted. Ted hadn't come with us. In fact, we'd hardly seen him since the execution. Unavoidably detained. But he had made the coffin. Suppose it had been the least he could do when he'd been such a Handy-Andy and Willing-Willy when it came to creating the instrument of execution. Ted the Yes. His eagerness to please. His chirpy 'Definitely!' His happy-go-lucky 'No problem!' All just a front for the terrible cynicism, and probably anger, which stalked his soul. A cynicism which frankly couldn't care – but which could bend with the wind, and tug the appropriate forelock when necessary. The present was all that mattered to Ted. The past was done and the devil could take tomorrow.

Only the past wasn't done. It never is. Remind me to mention somewhere in this rambling mess of a diary Little Ted's bedtime prayers …

*

Skarit was approaching. He'd been laughing with some of the guards who accompanied us. Tear-Sing walked alone but managed to communicate anger to all within a radius of one hundred miles of us. In a more populated area, this could have blighted the lives of millions. As it was, those affected must have comprised about eighty living souls, a few pharaohs, and those in between the living and the dead like desert tour operators. It was odd to be anticipating keenly another chat with the bullying, reckless and remorse-free monster who was Skarit. But when the alternative was Dalip …

'It would be best if you gave up now,' said Skarit encouragingly.

'Throw it all in, you mean?'

'Yes. You have no place here in the desert. You are broken, crippled souls, living out a little fantasy –'

'It's quite a large fantasy, actually. As fantasies go –'

'You're not related to T. E. Lawrence, by any chance?'

'Sorry?'

'T. E. Lawrence,' he said smugly.

'Er …'

'Lawrence of Arabia.'

'Ah!'

'Such a bright star in the desert firmament. You seem to like history. So I assumed you would know all about him.'

'Not *all* about him. I know his real name was Peter O'Toole, of course, but then everyone knows that.'

'Very amusing. But the joke of a disintegrating man, who thought, like Lawrence, that he could save the Arab world.'

'I have many failings, Skarit, but believing I can save people is not one of them.'

'Lawrence thought he could save people. You have seen the film?'

I had. In fact whisper it quietly in the corridors of faith, but I'd earned a few pounds for giving some time to one of David Lean's research team.

'It was a Sandhurst favourite,' continued Skarit.[9] 'Such valour, such inner strength, such promise. But when he limped home to England in 1919, he couldn't even save himself. Lawrence, the man who could out-ride, out-walk, out-shoot, outlast them all, revered guerrilla leader of the Arab community! He limped home. Broken.'

'What broke him?' I asked with not a little self-interest, feeling a lot like Humpty-Dumpty in his declining years myself.

'Maybe it started with the rape.'

'What rape?'

'You mean the historian doesn't know? Or are you just a specialist in sixteenth-century Germany? You should study military history. That's real history. That's the history which changes things. He was raped by Turkish soldiers when captured in 1917. Rape is good for that.'

'Good for what?'

'For breaking the spirit.'

'Oh I see. Well, how nice that it's good for something. Every cloud has a silver lining, eh?'

I was beginning to miss Dalip.

'Especially with the family present. That is very good. I have seen that. Very powerful.'

We walked for a while in silence. I suspected he wasn't finished yet. I suspected he had an advantage he wanted to press home, to stuff down my throat, to beat me with, towards submission. I wasn't wrong.

'You see, Abbot, gone are the days when torture was about gaining information. Oh, occasionally it is, but that is small-time. No, today torture has a larger brief. It is to destroy personality. So people don't die. It is just that they can no longer function as people. Your God is going to need to be a very good healer.'

'That is the rumour.'

'Humiliating and hurting the ones they love. That is best in my experience. Rape the mother in front of the husband and children. Rape the children in front of the husband and wife. Degrade. Debase. And watch the flower of life wither. It is very good. Not that the soldiers who raped Lawrence had thought all this through. They just wanted their pleasure, and good luck to them. But without knowing it, they were prophets. They were seers of abuse, pointing the way to future generations. That sort of thing makes me laugh.'

'I'm not surprised. I was finding your story a bit of a rib-tickler myself.'

'But I haven't finished my story yet.'

'No.'

'He's only half-broken. Our hero. Only half-broken.'

'Is he?'

'Yes. He can still get up and carry on, you see. There's more to come. More of Lawrence to be broken.'

'But maybe that's enough for tonight, daddy.'

'What did you say?'

'I said, maybe that's enough for tonight, daddy.'

'Why do you say that?' snapped Skarit, suddenly tense, smelling a threat in the air. *'Why did you say that?'*

'It was a plea. Recognise it? Recognise it from way back? What songs were sung to you in *your* cradle, Skarit?'

Skarit brooded a while. He brooded with his chest, with his gut where his true energy lay. Slowly, he regained control, regained mastery.

'After the rape came the terrible "loss of control". That was an incident which haunted desert Lawrence with a vengeance.'

'A loss of control is hardly a great sin.'

'After watching a Turkish massacre of sixty women and children, he retaliated in kind. Gave a "no prisoners" order. "The best of you brings me the most Turkish dead." Those were his words.'

'I see.'

'He wanted to be a good man. Like you. He wanted to be a good man. He wanted his life to mean something. But he finished his life in a desperate search for – what's the word? Penance? He liked to be degraded. He paid for the humiliation, travelled miles for it. All over London town. Towards the end, Abbot Peter, all Lawrence of Arabia wanted was to be whipped. The man who could out-ride, out-walk, out-shoot, outlast them all – he wanted to be whipped. Surprisingly, that wasn't in the film, but then who wants the truth? A broken spirit indeed. I don't think you will end your life much more happily –'

'We're nearly there,' I said.

'Nearly where?'

'The Place of the Graves.'

'The dead have no place, Abbot Peter. No place, no

future. Still, we allow you your silly religious games on this occasion.'

'How kind. So you won't mind if we pretend eternity, then? And we'll be as brief as we can ...'

*

I'd been increasingly conscious of the brooding present of Tear-Sing during the last few minutes. Constantino though was having a marvellous time – all toothless grin and jollity. He was travelling in the jeep next to the coffin. It was a four-hour journey by foot to the Place of the Graves. Constantino had wanted to walk it. Skarit had said he couldn't come. Carol had said why couldn't he travel in the jeep? Skarit had said okay. Carol stood up to Skarit. He seemed to respect her for it. He enjoyed the fear he created in people. But he also seemed to like those who stood their ground, treated him as an equal. His relationships with me were less cordial. He sensed that most of me was inside and therefore unseen and therefore a danger that could not always be anticipated and prepared for. In the fight for survival, Skarit needed to be prepared for *all* contingencies. He liked all the cards to be on the table.

*

'I don't want to talk with you, Abbot Peter.'

'It's not compulsory, Tear-Sing.'

'We talked before about understanding.'

'We did.'

'You don't understand. You are right.'

'Thank you. It's nice to be right sometimes.'

'But that is not the main problem. You have a deeper problem. You cannot feel. That is your deeper problem. There is no sense in me that you *feel* what I feel. You cannot make that leap, that connection.'

'Not doing very well, am I?'

'I can't help my mood.'

'No.'

'I can't help my darkness.'

'No.'

'I can't help the sense of desolation as beauty, love and hope seem to pass me by with eyes averted.'

He paused. I remained silent in my uselessness.

'But you can't feel that, can you? You try to help me understand it with my brain. To *explain* it. But you can't feel it. And if there is no feeling, there is no healing. You cannot be my healer. Maybe no one can. Maybe no one can feel with me. Maybe no one can bear that burden.

★

Gauguin left his Paris banking house and his wife, watched his small son starve, and himself died in 'nakedness and ecstasy' because he had discovered paint. Paint had been a dangerous enchantment for Gauguin, just as the desert had been a dangerous enchantment for me. In the early days, its sparseness and lack of consolation had been as gracious to me as a lover's caress, and its vastness a lavishing of liberty on my gasping, choking soul. But in the hot cold light of day the 'dangerous enchantment' was looking ever more like a 'stupid infatuation'. The sublimity of former times was AWOL.

There is a thin line between the desert, where we are stripped, and the wasteland, where we are destroyed, and the boundary is never clear. There is no large checkpoint to be crossed with much filling in of forms and checking of passports. There is no large sign saying: 'You are now leaving the desert.' There is no neon-lit information centre to help you make the most of the wasteland. No. The borderline is a master of disguise, adept at anonymity. The last step in the desert looks and feels very much like the first step in the wasteland. And the second step is very similar to the first. Thus the traveller tends to have walked some distance before the realisation dawns that here is a bleak place with no clear paths of return.

So how far have I walked? My life had always been a fine balance between a sense of futility and a sense of love. Now, I was afraid it was just futility. I looked at Constantino, as if to confirm it all. He was looking worried on his jeep throne. Here was an alien environment, and within him, he had no tools to interpret. Memory, and therefore possibility, was long gone. His travelling searching spirit, his delightful creativity, now just a tired sequence of semi-automatic responses. His sieve-like brain leaked information with pathetic speed. Constantino was a man disappearing into the blizzard of his own mind never to return; caught in a terrible swirling, a relentless dragging down, a terrifying vortex of drift. He grabbed at the flotsam of life's memories. He was trying to keep hold. Trying to keep hold. Trying to. Trying. Tired. Adrift. Falling. Losing. Fog. Trying. Dying. Alive but dying ...

Stage Four of stress is not being able to find the ladder. Anywhere. Any sort. No ladders for love nor money. I think I'd got there now, as we walked to the Place of the Graves, crucified quietly on the chill and seeping nails of futility. 'Doctor, doctor – I have only fifty-nine seconds to live!' 'All right, all right – sit down and I'll see you in a minute.'

*

Being slightly unsure of my own lines now, I leant on the past and pretended eternity through the words of St

Augustine. We had reached the Place of the Graves. We had dug. We now stood in a small circle. Some stepped forward to touch the coffin. Dalip knelt and held it. It wasn't so much lowered into the ground then, as pushed. Not very graceful, but alternatives were limited, and the soldiers certainly weren't helping. We then piled rocks on top of it and, as I say, I grabbed at the holy flotsam of another era:

> we shall rest and we shall see;
> we shall see and we shall love;
> we shall love and we shall praise.
> behold what shall be in the end,
> and shall not end.

Maybe. It would be some story if it was true. In the meantime, for all of us, even if there wasn't eternity, there was tomorrow. Probably. And tomorrow for me would start with sex.

CHAPTER FIVE

The Heavens Unopened

'I had sex with Sanjay the night before he died.'

Pause. Quite a long one. No eye contact. Having established I had no secret hot line to the outside world, Skarit had allowed Carol and me to meet in my study. We had to share it with the absurd gun at the window, which sat there ready for a war which didn't exist and an enemy which had long gone home. But then absurdity and self-delusion were scarcely strangers to my study.

'He'd been under close guard since the midday meal. I was responsible for him. The guards were at the end of the corridor. But I was his main link with the world. We talked. We talked about many things, for two or three hours. Then he cried and I held him. He sobbed. He calmed down after a while. We sat. And then, suddenly, he asked me.

'And you said yes.'

'I didn't say anything. We just had sex.'

Pause.

'I normally keep a fairly tight lid on these things.'

Pause.

'It's a weakness I have. Always have had. And death is one of the triggers it seems. Proximity to it, funerals, that sort of thing.'

Pause.

'I can't live with myself afterwards, of course.'

Pause.

'Which is why I'm here. I have to speak it. Not that you can help in any way.'

Pause. It was reassuring to have this confirmed. Just when I was in danger of thinking I might actually be doing something good, it was heart-warmingly affirming to be told that I wasn't. Nor could I. Ever.

'It is as though I have a cellar beneath my house,' continued Carol. 'It's where I keep the uncontrolled. Safe. Boarded down. I don't think I know the half of what's down there probably. But upstairs I'm a good girl. A very good girl. Sometimes I'm such a good girl that I even forget the cellar's there. Most of the time.

But sometimes the floor melts. It's actually quite terrifying. But quite exciting too. It melts away. And the uncontrollable breaks out. I'm not a good girl then. Not until the floor is back in place. I don't really know what to do.'

Carol looked at me for the first time. And for a brief moment, there was a pleading in her eyes. Behind the brisk, decisive, strong, reforming zealous leader's eyes, there was pleading. Not for long, mind. Normal service was soon resumed.

'I don't want answers, of course. I know the answers – floor reconstruction is nearing completion.'

Of course. Which just goes to show that knowing the answers is no answer at all. It was the questions Carol should have been considering. Questions like: 'Why did I build this cellar in the first place? How does it affect the way I treat people? What am I going to do with my disgust at daddy's behaviour? And how does it all affect my pictures of God?' Instead of the questions, however, she continued with some instructions.

'So please don't tell me the story of Jesus and the woman caught in adultery.[10] I know it already. I don't need to hear it again. And apart from anything else, he told her to sin no more. He told her not to do it again.'

'I wasn't going to tell you that story,' I said, feeling

heavily judged, not merely before I'd committed the crime, but before the notion of it had even entered my head.

'It's over-used. And he does tell her not to do it again. We forget that.'

Pause. A longer one. Not visible from the moon; not seeking equality with one of Jane Austen's sentences. But long enough to tell the discomfort. And it was true. After sending away all potential stone-throwers, all the rent-a-judge mob who gather at the scene of any happening, Jesus had said to the woman: don't do it again. He'd said he didn't condemn her. But he'd also said, don't do it again.

'And you see, I probably will,' said Carol. 'I probably will do it again. Or I might, anyway.'

'Yes. That story *is* a bit of a tease, isn't it? Leads the woman to the edge of grace. Allows her to look, feel, smell and touch a glorious freedom. And then snatches it all away. We're allowed to play with the toy, and then suddenly Jesus gets all moody, takes it back and says, "That's mine and I'm off now." Rather unfair, really. Because as you say, you probably will do it again. What we're confessing one week, we'll probably be confessing the next as well. Our compulsions are fairly predictable. Yes, I think I'm joining you. It's not fair.'

Carol's tone instantly changed. Her back straightened, her shoulders broadened, her neck became more rigid, and suddenly we were a million miles from the awkward yet gentle surveying of wreckage. We were now back in the lecture hall of debate and argument. The cellar ceiling was complete.

'I don't see it as unfair of Jesus. No – I wasn't saying it was unfair. People have to know where they stand; what they can and cannot do. People are very quick these days to declare things "unfair". Rather too quick in my view. No – I think it was very sensible of Jesus –'

A great weariness overcame me, and Jesus being tarred with the epithet 'sensible' was only part of the problem. Jesus? Sensible?? It was like calling the Sahara sandy. It was just so inadequate that it was *worse* than being wrong. The Eternal God who inhabits the dark places of the universe and calls into being that which is not; the seeping Creator Spirit who holds the galaxies as a toy, and the Infinite as a window box – this God did not take human form in order that we might be more *sensible.* If that were the extent of God's ambitions, then the angels would have been singing that 'Unto us this day is born a school teacher, who though lacking imagination, should at least ensure that we all behave a bit better.' That would have fired the shepherds to awe-filled devotion, eh? I can hear them now, exclaiming on the hillside: 'Behold! A child who is to become a worthy if slightly dull lecturer in rules, morals and etiquette! Let us go and worship this child and even now begin to pull our socks up a little, as he suggests!'

But then maybe for Carols the world over Jesus was, above all else, a teacher, and salvation a divine list of dos and don'ts ...

Still, it wasn't just the epithet 'sensible' that drove me from the room. I needed to leave on other grounds. Grounds like diminished responsibility. I needed to walk, to wander, drift, be aimless, to be useless. I needed to express my deepest calling which was to go forth and experience the terrible futility of it all. When concepts have run their course, you enter a very dark night indeed. When you've seen through everything, there's no celebration. Just a terrible mist.

'Carol, sometimes it's better just to enjoy the wreckage for a while,' I said with a sigh.

This was a door-handle statement. The saying of something very important as we leave, because it's safe then. We have an exit.

'Wreckage can be a very beautiful thing,' I continued. 'In fact, sometimes the wreckage is better than the shiny original. In your case, Carol, it's a lot better. If you don't mind me saying so. And now I must go.'

And I did. I went. I suggested that Carol leave in her own time, but that I was leaving now. Which was really very hard for me, partly because I had seven more pieces of the jigsaw to place, and partly because a hundred Carols had passed my way, and I knew the pattern, and I knew what to say. I knew. I *knew* everything. But what was the point? Wisdom can guide but it can't change. And strangely enough, for people like Carol, it's the last thing they need to hear. Until they can distinguish between daddy and God, wisdom really is the last thing they need to hear. Before you can say 'Judge Jeffries' they will have turned it into a rule, and hit themselves with it.

So I left the room, and took my useless wisdom for a stroll. I don't know how Carol felt, but I wasn't particularly concerned. I felt I was due for some withdrawal after the past few days. Carols the world over pretended reasoned and rational thinking, and enjoyed the cut and thrust of keen debate. But unless the debate reached their gut, there was little point. Unless a bridge could be built across the chasm which separated their head and their gut, over which true religion could healingly pass, their stomach ulcers and digestive problems would continue, and they would continue to live with all the stress of the makeshift floor, holding at bay the turbulent and angry lava flow beneath.

Still, such things were not my problem. My problem was the huge futility. And frankly, the desert wasn't helping. Not at all. I was finding its body language most unhelpful. Its lazy arid sprawl was futility personified, mocking me at just discovering something *he'd* known for twenty thousand years.

'Futility?' he said wearily. 'You haven't seen the *half* of it yet, young sir. Not the *half* of it ...'

'Thank you for that,' I said.

*

And then, the beginning of the end of this little story. I think, on reflection, it probably was. Or certainly a prelude to the beginning of the end, in as much as anything has a beginning, and anything has an end. And it started in the courtyard. I was sitting in the shadow, watching everything in general and nothing in particular. My vision was walled-in in every way. This meant that I couldn't see the postman approaching through the deep valley and burning sun with three significant letters in his hands. They would have their moment. But in the meantime, they weren't the message. No. The message on this occasion was not to be read, but to be seen and heard. The beginning of the end was about to be acted out in a piece of courtyard drama. On stage as the curtain opened were two soldiers, loitering by the wall painting of Abbot Nisteron, idly defacing his exploits with an army knife. Enter Constantino the Boy, stage right.

He was a-wandering. This means he must have slipped his minder. There was always someone keeping an eye, but from personal experience, you only had to blink and he was gone, voyaging into the unknown, seeking the past, seeking the places remembered, and waiting for his father who'd be along to collect him soon. He could be sure of that. He was stumbling gap-toothed across the courtyard, hunched and slow, yet still the restless butterfly soul who couldn't quite stay still. He approached the two soldiers who were abusing the good Abbot Nisteron and other assorted minor saints. Constantino told them he was eighty-seven. They couldn't understand. They laughed awkwardly at this daft old specimen. Constantino smiled. Company. He pointed to the refectory and made a face to suggest that he wouldn't be going in there again in a hurry! They laughed at this comic little fellow. Then he asked them who they were. They laughed again. They couldn't understand. One then reached for his gun. He showed it to Constantino, and enacted out a shooting as if to show him what it was for. The other soldier played the captive with his hands in the air, pretending capture and surrender.

And then the milk began to turn. Constantino liked the joke with the gun. The shorter of the two soldiers then gave it to him. Placed the gun in his hands. He didn't want it. He was suddenly confused and uncomfortable. The soldier insisted. Insisted Constantino hold the gun. *You hold it!* The courtyard mockery was turning nasty. Constantino had stopped smiling. The soldiers laughed at the bent old man holding their gun, as they acted terror and pleading. Don't shoot, don't shoot! Constantino asked them to take him home and to tell his father. They couldn't understand. Constantino got bored with this game and dropped the gun in the sand. The shorter soldier, whose gun it was, stopped laughing, swore at him and hit him. Constantino went down. I sat and searched inside my detached self for the spark of spontaneous action. All I found was Isaiah: 'Oh that you would tear the heavens open and come down! Make the nations tremble at your presence!'[11]

There was one, however, to whom sharp and instant action was second nature. There was one better suited to be saviour here than I. I hadn't noticed Skarit. But he too had been watching. He stepped out of the shadow and barked a command. The young soldiers looked terrified. The one who had struck Constantino knelt. Skarit took a pistol. Held it to the back of his head. Oh my God. He shouted some more. The young soldier dribbled fear. Skarit pulled the trigger. It was a blank. With his boot, Skarit pushed the kneeling figure forward. He fell into his own vomit. Skarit shouted again, this time at the other soldier. Constantino was picked up in haste but carried with desperate care towards the accommodation wing. The boy on the ground was made to stand. Skarit circled him. Then quieter precise words were spoken. The boy bent nervously to pick up his gun, expecting another assault. It didn't come. Instead, he was called to attention and then dismissed. He walked bendy-legged and sick-stained away, eyes a-stare, and feeling the place where the gun had pressed his head, and so nearly blown his one-careless-owner brains. He could feel, but he'd never feel that place away; he could rub-a-dub-dub, and scrub-a-dub-dub, but he'd never rub it away; never feel away that metal-nozzled circle of fear, pressed hard and heartless against his fragile skull, bringing him to the very edge of the abyss. Only a boy. Trouble is, they'd dressed him as a soldier ...

I got up and walked towards Skarit. He hadn't seen me, hadn't realised I was there, and he looked shifty. I was not meant to have been a witness to this.

'Discipline,' he said.

'Liar,' I replied. And smiled. Was this the first hint of spring, on the bleak banks of the river out of Eden?

*

It is, of course, one of the classic movements of the Christian life. The move from Hope to Desperation. It seemed a suitably festive theme as we sat in the chapel for evening prayer, on the first day of Advent. The shedding of absurd hope; the putting on of a deep desperation. The sort that cries out with Isaiah: 'Oh that you would tear the heavens open and come down!'

There was a remarkable stillness that night among the gathered. Bernadette was finding it slightly hard to settle, but the others sat stony-still and intense in the simple circle. Tear-Sing knelt on one of the prayer stools, and Dalip sat with his arm around Constantino, who seemed subdued. Carol had asked to light the first of the twenty-four candles which would lead us to the season of Christmas. She had also foregone her usual seat, and sat instead by the empty seat that had been Sanjay's. Ted the Yes was a surprising presence, standing by the door, but for the moment at least, choosing not to run. Another surprising presence was Skarit, inhabiting the shadows of the east end.

The service of the Blessing of Light was a simple service, and we started with the familiar responses.

PRIEST: Your Word, O God, is a lantern to our feet and a light to our path. The light and peace of Jesus Christ be with you all.

PEOPLE: And also with you.

PRIEST: Let us give thanks to the Lord our God.

PEOPLE: Who is worthy of all thanksgiving and praise.

PRIEST: Blessed are you, Sovereign God, creator of light and darkness! As evening falls, you renew your promise to reveal among us the light of your presence. May your word be a lantern to our feet, and a light to our path, that we may behold your glory coming among us. Strengthen us in our stumbling weakness and free our tongues to sing your praise, Father, Son and Holy Spirit.

PEOPLE: Blessed be God forever!

And so the liturgy went on, carrying us in its strong and ancient arms. Its grip on the lives of us all seemed fairly complete. And then came the lesson from Holy Scripture, brought to us by Dalip. Isaiah crying out for what Jacob was given free: the tearing open of heaven. I then stood up to share some thoughts on the matter.

'It is, of course, one of the classic movements of the Christian life,' I said, 'and one we particularly need to attend to in the Season of Advent: the movement from Hope to Desperation. There is really nothing more pressing or essential. That we turn aside from foolish optimism, and gaze into the abyss. And feel as Isaiah felt when he called out, cried out, screamed out: "Oh that you would rend the heavens open and come down!"

'Like the Buddha. It wasn't until he was twenty-nine that he screamed, of course. Before that, so legend whispers, he enjoyed the gilded life of a palace prince, with beautiful wife and beautiful son. Then one day, he ventured out into the real world, and encountered sickness, old age and death. He encountered even more devastatingly the horror of one whose answers suddenly don't seem very adequate in the face of the questions. It was the start of his spiritual journey, which focused throughout on the strong need to come to grips with the miserable human condition.

'We may not want to follow the Buddha in his

conclusion that the answer to human suffering lies in ridding the body of all desire; that true hope lies in not hoping for anything. There is much stoic wisdom contained therein. Much discipline. Much depth. But no hope. Which is a shame. Because call me Mr Sentimental, but sometimes it's the glimmer of hope which helps me to get out of bed in the morning.

'But may God spare us all not only from untimely death but also from the hope as portrayed on a Christian wall calendar I was recently sent by a missionary organisation. One might have gleaned from this sad publication that the truest Christian hope lies in puppy dogs doing sweet and amusing things in baskets; that the place God really wants to be is by a chirpy little mountain stream during an alpine spring; and that the angels tend to like their sunsets golden and their water mirror calm. In other words, that God is as paralysed by suffering as a desert hare in headlights, as frightened and clueless as the rest of us frankly, and needs to escape into the kitsch, the facile and the pretty in order to survive. Let us hope with all our hearts that there is a generously proportioned place in hell for all who publish such nonsense; for all who misapply the Bible verses which accompany them and for all who pack and seal up the calendars to send to people like myself.

'The move from Hope to Desperation: such an important movement in the Christian life. From a Christian calendar hope, limply rooted in avoidance and denial, to a desperation which knows that the dogs of dislocation, anxiety and fear sleep not only on our doorstep but within our very selves. May God in his kindness lead us from a wistful hope based on ignorance and vague imaginings to a strong desperation born of experience – experience of the world, of myself. Even of God. Let each of us reach that place which is called the pit, the end. Yes, I think so. The place where we too scream with Isaiah, "Oh that you would tear the heavens open and come down."

'And yet. And yet Lord, you are our father. Isaiah can't quite shake it off. He's shouted his head off, vented his spleen all over the place. He's as angry as a wasp with a headache, but he still can't quite escape the family ties. You are our father. I'm sorry you are. *You're* probably sorry you are. But tough. You are. You are our father. You hide your face from us, but you are our father. Our integrity is in rags, and that feels like a Thursday afternoon in February frankly, yet you are our father. Yes. We'd like to call the whole thing off. But we can't. We're stuck with you. You're stuck with us.

'And so the rumour *is*, campers, believe it or not, that

there is a path beyond the base camp of desperation. For there is a father. But before we dare seek that path, we'll need to make it to the base camp itself. Maybe you have already. From hope to desperation. May God be in your Advent journey. And forgive me if I've sounded too triumphalistic.'

As always when I preached, I'd been talking to myself. Others, if they were listening, could take from it what they willed. But it really wasn't for them. I couldn't imagine anybody being very seriously blessed by my verbal indulgences, and for me the classic definition of preachers remained as 'those who talk in other people's sleep'. Yes. I had long since given up trying to change the world. The idea of being changed myself was still quite intriguing though. Utterly impossible, of course. But intriguing.

★

And tomorrow? It was to be all about the arrival of Abbot Donaldo. But then again it wasn't, inasmuch as by the evening office, the abbot would loom extraordinarily small on all our horizons. 'Overtaken by events' is, I think, the phrase. But for the moment, the big night sky, the deep desert dark, the chill, and the silence. And maybe, if God was good, the grace to reflect on the day that had been. As I reflected, I wrote this:

I'm feeling sort of tired
Weary as the winding road
Dry as the desert and the dune
Empty as that big white shiny moon

The merry-go-round's closed down
The man in the mirror won't smile
There's a hush in the House tonight
The audience is looking less than polite

The funfair's all deserted
The one where I used to play
Music Hall is dying you see
But tell me, what is it that's dying in me?

I'm feeling sort of tired
Weary as the winding road
Dry as the desert and the dune
Empty as that big white shiny moon …

CHAPTER SIX

Beyond the Pipe Organ

THERE are two things worse than a full-scale military invasion of your premises. The first is having the builders in. The second is Harmful Religion.

The Worst-Case Universe is not a good place, of course. It's a bad place. A terrible place where your worst fears are always realised; where that which you most dread always occurs; a regular house of horrors inhabited by sick outcomes, awful experiences, unbearable situations and lethal dilemmas. But give them their due. Even amongst *them* – the sick, the awful, the unbearable and the lethal – Harmful Religion is something of a moral outcast. For even they know that you have to draw the line somewhere. Even they reluctantly acknowledge that, occasionally, enough is enough. But Harmful Religion doesn't, you see. It never acknowledges that. Enough is never enough. It's ambitions are total. It believes in itself too much. It's just *too* dangerous, *too* lethal, hurts too many people, destroys too many personalities, warps too many souls, divides too many nations. And causes too many rather poor songs to be written. No wonder, then, that it tends to get shunned even in the corridors of the Worst-Case Universe. Harmful Religion is the sort of thing which makes one misty-eyed and remember-when nostalgic for the Black Plague and mass famine.

It needs a leader, of course. Someone to organise the illness. Some damaged soul hell-bent on creating a system or a community in which his sickness can be called health. As far as I remember, Abbot Donaldo arrived at the tenth hour on the following day …

*

Oh dear. Was that too obvious? It wasn't meant to sound quite like that, but then again, it probably was, because I find it very difficult to keep the bile inside under wraps. Anyway, I love tradition and it's certainly traditional to bad-mouth rivals, even in the desert. *Particularly* in the desert, in fact, where the ill spirit of competition among leaders has a fine pedigree. Certainly Macarius in the fourth century was a craftsman at it, in his own religious way. Did a leader in a neighbouring monastery eat only a pound of bread in Lent? Then he, Macarius, would eat only a crust. Did another leader eat no cooked food during this season of abstinence? Then he would eat raw herbs for seven years. He knew how to twist the knife, old Macarius.

He once went in disguise to the monastery of Tabenna where the abbot was the great Pachomius. Macarius planned to teach 'the great Pachomius' a thing or two, and lesson one was Austerity. So throughout Lent, he stood himself in a corner of the courtyard, neither eating nor drinking, neither kneeling nor lying nor sleeping nor speaking. Instead, he prayed silently while plaiting palm leaves and, just to avoid ostentation – God forbid! – he would eat a little raw cabbage on Sundays.

The reaction of the brethren at Tabenna was unanimous. They were unanimously infuriated by the emaciated and ridiculous presence of this mystery visitor who seemed to bring them all into contempt. Dressing up my own inner disturbance as goodness may make *me* feel better, but it's really very exhausting and depressing for everyone else. A delegation was formed, and old Pachomius was told that either this pious misery went – or the rest of them did.

After due meditation and prayer on the matter, which

must have lasted a good two minutes, Pachomius decided to go and see him. He approached the gaunt saint with due humility and deference, and asked if they might talk in his private oratory. Macarius, sensing an admirer, was happy to oblige. Once there, Pachomius gently rebuked him for disguising his true identity from them. There was really no need. Such game-playing was unnecessary by so revered a spiritual leader as Macarius. Macarius, who was definitely warming to this criticism, was then *thanked* by Pachomius. Thanked greatly, 'for you have clouted the ears of these youngsters of mine and put the conceit out of them. Now therefore return to the place from which you came: we have all been sufficiently edified by you. Oh – and pray for us.'

Marvellous stuff. 'Get lost, you sad, sad man' never sounded so fine. And Macarius fell for it hook, line and sinker. Macarius mistook a knee in the groin for a royal visit and left feeling on top of the world. The desert is not just a school of prayer. It is also a school of diplomacy. By the grace of God, Pachomius managed it with Macarius. But would I manage it with Donaldo? Abbot Donaldo of the Monastery of the Sacred Heart and Abounding Mercy. What a stupid name for a monastery in the first place ...

I needed only to think of his clothes to become irritated. His exquisite habit, which was a rich cream colour, and which hung so impressively from his shoulders, was emblazoned with a crown of thorns, dripping red, and a broken figure *à la* Macarius plaiting palm leaves. Who could help but be impressed by such stirring symbols of sacrifice and humility? It was rumoured to be five hundred years old and the very habit worn by Thasos the Good who was martyred by being thrown from the great rock on which the monastery of the Sacred Heart sat. In fact, I happened to know that the habit in question was designed by Abbot Donaldo himself and made, after seven sittings, by a rather exclusive tailor in Milan, with two spares, just in case his sacrifice and humility got a little grubby. I'm afraid I was sufficiently edified by Donaldo within thirty seconds of our meeting.

It would have helped if I'd known he was coming. It would have helped if I'd seen the letter announcing his arrival. But I didn't. And so I was unprepared, and one of the few things I've learnt about myself is that I am a better human being when I *am* prepared. Spontaneous goodness is not my strong suit. His letter was one of three which had arrived the previous day. It explained, as I subsequently discovered, that he was on his way back from inter-faith discussions in Cairo with the Grand Mufti, one of the most significant Muslim clerics in the country. The venue had been the university of Al-Azhar. I'd been there once, in the days when I was still up and coming. Marvellous place if you like that sort of thing. It trained imams and Muslim teachers and was possibly the oldest university in the world. The talks had been 'absolutely fantastic' of course. Things tended to be described in this way by Donaldo. Things were brilliant or amazing or remarkable or mind-blowing, without him ever really being able to put any substance behind or beneath these ecstatic declarations. Apart from when he was talking to grant-making bodies, of course, when the eventual substance was there for all of us to see and choke over. Tea-making facilities at the end of every corridor.

He'd then spent a 'completely delightful' few days with the Patriarch of the Coptic Church, at his monastery set in the desert of Wadi el Natroun. But now, coming over all Pauline, 'it was his strong desire to see his brothers and sisters in Christ at St James, before returning to the Sacred Heart'. He must want something.

As I say, however, the letter revealing all this had not yet reached me. The postman had delivered. A soldier had collected. But then the mail trail went cold. Our traditionally inefficient postal system had been replaced by a new sort of inefficiency which we obviously hadn't quite yet mastered. So when Donaldo arrived I was uninformed, unprepared and unhappy at being caught out and exposed for the loveless soul that I am. I reacted to him, you see – instead of responding to him. A rather sad eventuality, because reacting to people is not generally a very wholesome business. Common, but not very wholesome. And so my opening encounter with Donaldo wasn't very impressive.

*

Before that encounter, however, the *second* of the three letters *had* been opened. It had been opened by Carol. Not ripped open. She probably used a knife. Clean cut. But more important than the current state of the envelope were the contents of the letter inside.

*

Carol's chest was heaving in restless dilemma, letter in hand. I anticipated a struggle. I'd need a strong sense of the 'divine other' in the room, which is why I generally lit a candle when people came to call. A sign of a third party, listening, disturbing, creating – and loving. Unfortunately in this instance, we already *had* an 'other' in the room, and it was proving very hard to get rid of him. For Ted the Yes was trying to sell me a pipe organ.

'Just thought the chapel could do with some decent ivories, and I know this bloke –'

'Could we talk about it another time, Ted?' I asked, well aware of Carol's embarrassment.

'I was just standing in there the other night, during that prayer thing, and thinking that you might be able to use one, and my brother-in-law has just started this business –'

'We don't want a pipe organ at St James the Less, Ted. It's not an issue for us.'

'But you see what *I'm* talking about *isn't* a pipe organ. That's the whole point, Abbot. That's the nub. That's exactly what I'm saying. They're electronic, in fact. But they sound a dead ringer for the genuine. I mean, you *can't* tell the difference, I swear on my father's ashes –'

'This really isn't a very good time, Ted. Carol and I were just talking. Perhaps I could catch up with you later?' In another life, maybe.

'Built by craftsmen. Chosen by the discerning. That's what my brother-in-law says. I could get you the brochure. Or better still – now here's an idea, you'll like this – I could get him to come over and have a look-see. Nothing like having a third opinion.'

'There's nothing like bad breath either, but it doesn't mean I seek it out.'

'He could get over here next week, perhaps, bring a brochure and give the chapel a quick once-over.'

'We are occupied, you know.'

'I think I could swing it,' said Ted.

'Could you ask him to bring a ladder then?'

'Sorry?'

'Your brother-in-law. When he comes, could you ask him to bring a ladder? I'd be interested in one of those.'

'What? You still want a ladder in the chapel?'

'I still want a ladder in the chapel.'

'You should have said.'

The patience of Job finally buckled under the strain.

'Ted, I've *said* a thousand times. You've said yes a thousand times. You've done nothing about it a thousand times. A thousand times your yes has been a no. Please now at least do me the honour of not pretending you didn't know we wanted a ladder.'

'It's just that Dalip wants the ladder to stay with the gallows, so I thought fair's fair for the lad, had a rough time and all that, but that does leave us one ladder short, so to speak.'

One ladder short. My epitaph probably. 'Here lies

Peter the Fool. One ladder short of a divine encounter.' Shame, really.

'But I'll see Ricky and we'll sort one out. He's nearly finished on the fascia work. He'll be done by this afternoon, certainly. Definite. And if not by this afternoon, tomorrow. So the ladder won't be a problem. We'll have a nice ladder for you in the chapel. Tonight. We'll get it there tonight. I'll go and have a word now. How does that sound?'

It sounded like a bedroom long ago, described falteringly to me, which belonged to a little boy called Edward. His teeth were clean and he'd washed behind his ears like his mother said, because young Edward was learning to be convenient – convenient to his parents. They had enough on their plate, what with their 'disagreements'. They didn't need an inconvenient child as well. Ted didn't want to be inconvenient. But he was worried about some things, and frightened about some things, as little boys are when the shades lengthen and darkness comes, and tired eyes are rubbed, and things come unbidden to the mind.

'I'm a bit worried, mummy.'

'I have not got time for *your* worries, Ted. You know what to do with them.'

'Shall I put them under the carpet?'

'That's right. Imagine the big carpet. Imagine the big brush.'

Edward lay still with his eyes tight shut, imagining once again the carpet and the brush. He knew what to do. It was a familiar ritual. It was a big red carpet, like the one in the hall, but the brush was a strange-shaped one which he'd invented himself.

'And now lift that carpet up, and brush those worries under,' continued his mother, who was in a hurry. 'Out of sight and out of mind. Feel better?'

'Yes, mummy. Much better.'

'Good boy, Ted. Mummy's good boy.'

As Edward lay there in the dark, it felt good to have been so convenient, to have kept the peace and not to have been the cause of conflict or row. Perhaps one day he'd bring his parents together. Really together, so they were happy again, and laughter filled the silences. But at other times he was stood on a station platform. A train pulled in and his parents boarded. But the train was splitting here, and the carriages were uncoupled, and his parents were uncoupled and eased their way out of the station in different directions. And Edward didn't know which way to look or which way to wave or which way to cry ...

He did sometimes wonder what became of the

worries under the carpet. Did they disappear? Or did they just sit hidden, trapped in the darkness and the dust. And why when he brushed them under the carpet did so many return? How did they get out? He wanted to ask his mum that one but thought she might shout at him. And she had enough on her plate without *his* nonsense. So he didn't ask. He just said yes. And anyway, he was tired and sleep beckoned and in the morning, when the light came, it was always all right, and the station seemed a long way away.

Thirty-five years on, the carpet remained in place, and Ted had popped his head around the door of the refectory, where Carol and I were sitting, and started straight in about the organ. And so it came to pass that we discovered another 'couldn't' in Ted. He couldn't say no. That we knew. Neither, however, could he listen to an environment when he walked into it. Otherwise, he would have sensed straight away the mood and the struggle of the moment he had gate-crashed. But he missed it. Or ignored it. And so Ted the Yes became Ted the Very Inappropriate.

But then again, why not? Although he didn't know it, Ted was sick of being convenient. And slowly but surely, everyone else was paying.

*

Carol and I would have been in my study, of course, but four of the soldiers were playing backgammon there. I wished I hadn't known. It made concentration much more difficult. Half of me was committedly with Carol, certainly. But the other half was wondering whether they were disturbing the Sydney Opera House and related sky. I was particularly concerned about the sky.

'I hate that rat,' Carol had said as the scuttling started again in the cage across the room.

'Yes.'

'A completely unnecessary humiliation.'

'Indeed.'

'And how it affects Tear-Sing as he prepares the meals here, I don't know.'

Pause. Takes time for people to get around to what they want to say. Some never make it. But Carol did.

'I have been asked to chair the commission.'

I chair, you chair, we all chair. 'Chair' as a verb. Being a desert-dweller, and rather out of touch with the world's crumbling empires and disintegrating grammar, I was still getting used to that one.

'Really? Congratulations.'

'Thank you.'

'You must be pleased.'

'Yes, I am. Skarit gave me the letter this morning.'

'From the Archbishop of Canterbury?'

'The very same. Not your run-of-the-mill notepaper, this.'

'Indeed. Well, there are still one or two things the Church hierarchy does very well indeed.'

'And what, in your opinion, is the second thing?' asked Carol.

'I was being charitable, but I'm sure, given time, I could think of something.'

'I can't accept it, of course.'

'What? You mean there are *more* than two things the Church hierarchy does well?'

Never let it be said the desert doesn't spring its fair share of surprises.

'No. I mean I can't accept the offer. I can't chair the commission on liturgy. Not in my present state. I really don't feel that I can.'

'And why is that exactly?'

'I need hardly elaborate, Abbot. Even you must see that my present state leaves something to be desired. What I've done is quite unacceptable.'

'So you're not perfect.'

'I don't need reminding.'

'So you're not the messiah.'

'Hardly!'

'So why pretend that you are? There's no need. We have one already anyway. He's called Je–'

'That's not quite how I view it.'

'No?'

'I am a teacher.'

'Yes. And?'

'There is such a thing as setting a good example.'

'Absolutely.'

'I haven't set one, I'm afraid. I have failed very grievously in the setting of standards.'

'I see. So what are you saying? That you must be better than people to help people? That in order to teach, you must be morally superior to the pupils? Looks like I better hand my sheriff's badge in right away.'

'I think there are certain justifiable expectations laid on the teacher – yes, I do as a matter of fact. I think we teachers of the Faith should be examples of the Faith, certainly. I think it's fairly basic to the whole thing that we do set standards for others to strive towards, and keep to those standards ourselves. We must be dragon-slayers ourselves, if we're inviting others to take up the sword and enter the fight.'

'Oh dear.'

'Oh dear? What's that supposed to mean?'

'It just means "oh dear", really. But then you see, Carol, I'm a Christian.'

'So you say. The evidence may be thin, but you seem to keep saying it.'

'I'm a Christian, and so with St Paul, I live daily and knowingly with a large number of unslayed dragons, I'm afraid. I live daily with the truth that I do what I don't want to do. I want to choose good but find it extraordinarily difficult, and often impossible.'

'So how are you different?'

'I'm not. That's just the point. That's what I'm trying to say. Rather badly, as it happens, but trying anyway. Trying to say I'm not any different. But then I'm not a believer because of me. I'm not a believer because of the example I set. I'm a believer because of God. And that's a very different plate of couscous. It relocates the strain of existence – the strain which so destroys you.'

It was at this point that I remembered to light the candle.

'So you do mention God occasionally?'

'As little as possible, Carol. He's too precious. Too much of a mystery. But sometimes, it's really very hard not to, and this is one of those moments. Your atheism has driven me to it. The absurd strain you put yourself under has driven me to it.'

'I don't find it as hard as you to talk about God, actually.'

'No, you find it very easy. But you do find it hard to *experience* God.'

'I think the rules are fairly clear.'

'I've never doubted your experience of the *rules*, Carol. But the rules aren't God. Without wishing to state the obvious, God is God. There really are very large tracts of atheism in you, Carol.'

Pause. I became conscious again of the scuttle and scrape of the rat. I became conscious again of Constantino wandering alone into the blizzard: 'I'm going out now. I may be gone some time.' I became conscious again of the sheer futility of it all. I became conscious again of the devastating inability of any human being to change. I knew that for myself, of course. But I was rather looking forward, in my dotage, to being gloriously surprised by the change in others. From where I was sitting, however, Skarit the Rat, Ted the Yes, Tear-Sing the Sad, and Carol were pretty well bedded in for life.

'I find *you* telling *me* about vast tracts of atheism pretty hard to handle,' said Carol, almost tearful with anger.

Her father had made her stand and salute for the

national anthem. Whatever she was doing in the house Little Carol had to stop, stand and salute. Alcohol-permitting, he sometimes joined her, but not usually. Usually, he just sat and she stood and saluted alone. It was a good thing to do. She never questioned that. But it might have been nice if someone else was good with her. It might have been nice if *he* was good. There's an exhaustion in being good by yourself. And a terrible anger, if only it could be spoken. But that wouldn't be good. Better to stand. Better to salute. Show the way …

'Foolish words, no doubt, and for those you must forgive me, Carol. But I'm always surprised at how little people know about the Sahara desert. Yes? I mean, most people really do still imagine it to be mile upon mile of golden sandy dune. In fact, as you and I know, only about a tenth of it is actually sand. The rest is a rather rocky and brown wilderness, with huge mountainous outbreaks, alongside really quite extensive belts of fertile land. And there is snow on the mountains for half the year. Snow in the Sahara. And there is water everywhere fifty feet or so beneath the surface. Yet to most people, as I say, the Sahara is an undulating yellow of wispy wind-whipped sand.'

'I had a dull geography teacher too.'

'It's just that most believers think they are "endless Christians". That is their understanding of themselves. *Fully Christianised.* In terms of the Sahara – all sand! All saved! How little we know. How little we've experienced of ourselves, how little has been revealed to us. So much that is hidden. How very fortunate that very possibly there is an eternity to explore, not only the mystery who is God, but also the mystery who is our good selves, made in the image of God.'

Why was I saying this? I seemed to have been speaking for a very long time, particularly given the fact that Carol wasn't listening. And then I remembered.

'And that, of course, is the first calling of the teacher, Carol. Not to be better than the pupils. But to have explored further.'

*

'Abbot Donald! A surprise visit!'

'It's Donaldo, Peter. You're being naughty again. My name is Abbot Donaldo now, and I'd be pleased if you could remember that.'

'Of course. Donaldo. It *was* Donald. It's now *Donaldo.* I'm sure I'll get the hang of it soon. It's just so confusing when people change their names. Don't you find that?'

'I haven't *changed* it, Peter. I've *developed* it. Developed it within my divine calling.'

'Ah yes. *Developed* it. And very fine it sounds too. Worth, what? An extra £500,000 a year in funding?'

'You wouldn't be at all bitter, would you?'

'Oh, I expect so. As bitter as the strong black coffee of the Cairo street markets. But that doesn't mean I don't understand. I mean, call me a philistine, but the name Donald will always speak to me of a duck.'

'So you have said. More than once.'

'Have I? So predictable, me. But then, you could hardly have abbreviated it to Abbot Don could you? No. I can quite see that. You really can't have hundreds of Micks, Daves and Dons wandering about the desert. Much too informal. I think we'd all agree. Where's the respect? But Donaldo – well, that's brilliant. What a difference an "o" makes. Changes the whole persona. Master-stroke of image-making.'

'There's nothing wrong with a bit of image.'

'Like your wonderful habit, of course, with all that suffering and humility so prominently and colourfully displayed. Cuts out the need for personal holiness really. The image is almost effortlessly there. Reputation 5: Reality 0. Abbot Donaldo. Only been in the desert five minutes but already being spoken of as the successor to Father Anthony.'

'Your words.'

'Well, Carol said they were yours, actually.'

A weary smile from Donaldo, meaning who knows what? But certainly a glimpse of the depressive kept so at bay by the manic.

'The Patriarch sends his greetings,' he said.

'I am honoured.'

'I was just saying to him only yesterday, over the iced coffee, which was really very splendid – have you tried the Patriarch's iced coffee?'

'Not to my knowledge, no.'

'You should. You really should. If you're ever invited, seize the opportunity. It's startlingly good. Amazing. Brilliant. It's the tops – it really is.'

'You liked it then?'

'Oh yes. And you'd *love* it. You really would.'

I hated it when people presumed to bring me in on their escapism.

'But as I was saying,' continued Donaldo in full name-dropping flow, 'the Patriarch and I were talking, and I was telling him what a noble job you're doing here at, how can I put it? At one of the less *coveted* posts in the desert. But then, as you know, I personally think it's a wonderful little set-up here. I really do. A quaint charm all of its own. Fantastic. And if it is to go, and that's progress I suppose, then I for one will remember it very fondly.'

'What a relief that is for us all.'

'Another time and another place, and it could have been the Sacred Heart making way, but as it is – well, times have changed, Peter. Marketability. It's important. The Sacred Heart is very therapy-centred now, of course, and maybe that's the difference. Modules for self-actualisation, aromatherapy, face massage and reflexology, that sort of thing. And remarkably, we're finding the desert was never so popular.'

'Yes. I'm afraid we're still stuck on the old cross and resurrection story. And prayer of course. Fools to ourselves, really.'

'Impressed by your security firm, though. I wasn't expecting quite such a guard. Troubled by gate-crashers obviously. Not that I'd heard that keeping people *out* was a particular difficulty at St James. Rather the opposite in fact. Or perhaps they're here to keep people *in*?!'

Donaldo gestured in an amused fashion to the three surly youths in soldiers' outfits who had brought him to me and now stood together about five yards away. He was clearly unaware of our predicament.

'We are a community under some stress, Donald. You have been let in by these soldiers. Whether you will be let out is quite another matter.'

'What do you mean? Is this one of your little jokes?'

'We have been invaded, Donald. Taken over. Raped. Burgled. Frightened. Very frightened. We continue our life here as normally as possible, as normally as is allowed, but there is military rule. The lunatics have taken over the asylum. There has been terror. There has been an execution. Sanjay the Mouse. He was hanged.'

'Oh,' said Donald, with a sudden hollowness of the eyes.

He was more sorry than anyone could know, because little Donald didn't want any more pain. When little Donald had gone to bed at night in Philadelphia he'd wondered a terrible thing. He'd lie in the room that never felt quite his own and wonder if his mother hated him. Maybe she did, because it was so often no. So much denied. So little given. Why? She was a single parent, but there were lots of those, and a lot of them couldn't do enough for their children. Look at Sally's mum. And they didn't have a huge amount of money, but that wasn't rare, and it didn't mean you couldn't be generous sometimes. Gerry's mum was, and they had much less. It was a terrible pain for a little person, in a small room, who was in the hands of a big person, with very little redress.

Later, when little Donald grew up, he discovered his

mother had a very particular sort of religion. It wasn't a religion that believed in nurturing; it believed in many things but not in giving in to the desires of a child. But by that time little Donald was long gone, in every sense. Gone from the place of control by another; gone from the place of pain inside; gone from little Donald. There was just Big Donald now, and the frenetic pursuit of the pleasurable, the fun, the stimulating and the tasty. Big Donald would go anywhere, anytime – except back to pain. Nothing would induce him to go back there. Big Donald was manic, bubbling, planning and travelling because he didn't want to taste the tears on his pillow again. No one would deny him anything now.

'Yes. I'm afraid we're a long way from the wow of the Patriarch's iced coffee. And frankly, we're looking for something a little more substantial than a module in aromatherapy and a decent facial rub, nice though it sounds. Because it's not just our long term which is uncertain. It's our every hour. The rat scuttles and we wait, Donald. We wait. And the waiting finds you out, wouldn't you say? Not the success. That finds nothing out. But the waiting. That finds you out with a vengeance. It's found me out anyway ...'

I paused. An unexpected touch of reality had entered

our pathetic dialogue. Amid the unedifying verbal combat, the submission to long-term personal prejudice, and the mere reaction to each other, I had unintentionally tapped into my own sense of vulnerability and desperation. And probably his too. And so I was responding, not reacting. It was of course a better place to be, a good deal more healthy. And not a place I visited enough. I just hadn't wished to visit it in the presence of my old foe Donaldo. But since I had started, I decided to finish.

'So when you ask me if we are troubled by gatecrashers, the answer is, yes, we are. Greatly troubled. Ripped apart by them in fact. But we are even more troubled by ourselves, I think. Even more troubled by the people we are, by the people we have become. I think so.'

Another pause. A hint of recognition in Donaldo's eyes? Maybe. Or maybe just the effortless appearance of listening, even though Donaldo had never listened to anyone in his life. He couldn't afford to. And there wasn't the internal space anyway. Still, he was a better man than I, no question about that, and he'd travelled a long way, and needed looking after. Sometimes even more pressing than eternity is a strong drink and a good meal.

'Let me find you some refreshment. And then guard-willing, we will wander the monastery together. And who knows – maybe God will save us both.'

And a few hours later, maybe God did. It was to be a strange epiphany though …

CHAPTER SEVEN

A Good Story

THERE was something of the slow motion about it all. And a large slice of the inconsequential too. It started out as really very ordinary. The afternoon lethargy of the courtyard prevailed. The stage was quiet. The audience tired. The sky was blue. The heat was intense. It was time for rest or simple reading in your cell. Being myself largely through with words, it was the time when I usually cleaned the lavatories and sinks in the wash house. But patterns had been broken over the past few days.

And then Carol appeared, with Constantino. They went together into the refectory. She'd taken him there yesterday afternoon, to spend time in the kitchens. Once there, the blizzard within had seemed to lessen apparently as Constantino had recognised where he was, and complained about the state of the work surface, tut-tutting to his heart's content, which was an encouraging sign of life. Sometimes complaints are.

Donaldo and I were standing by the gallows, standing looking at the world snooze in the afternoon lull, content with Sister Death at our shoulders. This was another sign of life. For Donaldo wasn't strong on death – his or anyone else's. But the gallows seemed all right. He wasn't moving on for once. We'd toured and we'd walked. Even the Sacred Heart was having trouble with their builders apparently. It was good to know that there were some absolutes in life.

Then into the afternoon drift came Tear-Sing, walking quickly. Very quickly. His head was down, avoiding all eye-contact, but he did look behind once, as if to check that he wasn't being followed. He was holding something in his right hand. If it wasn't a gun, it looked very like it. But what was Tear-Sing doing with a gun? He too went into the refectory. The inconsequential and the ordinary was becoming less so, for Tear-Sing didn't usually hurry anywhere, quite the opposite, and then there was Skarit running across the courtyard towards the refectory. He was slightly overweight but brisk and military-muscled and in the door before I suggested to Donaldo that we go over and see what was happening.

There was shouting inside. Tear-Sing and Skarit initially, but then Carol's voice. As we got closer, words became clearer. And we listened.

'Stand back!' shouted Tear-Sing. 'Stand away! Understand me. I will fire! I am not afraid! I am not afraid!'

He was going to kill himself. He'd been on the brink of it for a long time.

'Drop it,' said Skarit.

There was a pause.

'Drop it.'

'No,' said a weeping Tear-Sing. 'No, I won't. I don't need to listen to you now. Not any longer. I've listened before, remember? Face down in the sand I listened to your stupid taunts. But not now. Not any longer. No. I think it is time that you suffered maybe.'

Was the gun pointed at *Skarit?* What was he doing in there? Had he gone mad? If he shot Skarit we'd *all* be hanged. If we were lucky.

Suddenly, Carol's voice. I'd forgotten she was there.

'Give it to him,' she said firmly. 'Give it to him, Tear-Sing. While you have the chance.'

Give what to who? And then a scuffle. The sound of

a bench going over, I think, tables scraped. The grunt and the yelp of struggle, and then the gunshot. Loud. Very loud. Tear-Sing screamed. Another gunshot. Silence. Another gunshot. Heavier silence.

'I think he's dead by now,' said Carol.

'Yes, he is dead,' said Skarit.

I turned to Donaldo and our eyes met as the last two survivors on planet earth, which in the end is how all of us should meet. And then slowly, the refectory door opened, pushed by Skarit's foot, and he came out, carrying the limp body of Tear-Sing in his arms. They were strong arms, holding Tear-Sing in effortless safety. It was a bit late for safety now though. He stood in the cloister, as though in contemplation, and then, becoming aware of us, carried him toward us. He held him as if he were a child, looking both of us in the eye with a long look. Slowly he lowered the body onto the ground but continued to support Tear-Sing's upper body on his lap. There was a lot of blood. And then Carol, pale as the winter's sun, came out with Constantino.

'Well the mayfly only lives for two and a half hours,' he said.

There was blood on Carol too. But she seemed most concerned with Constantino.

'He'll be all right,' said Skarit.

'I hardly think so,' she replied, looking at the old man by her side.

Skarit then signalled to Donaldo, to take hold of Tear-Sing, in all his bloody glory. So now Donaldo was kneeling in the dirt, smeared by the body mess.

'You, Peter, come with me.'

Skarit nodded towards the refectory door. He was confident, in charge. He was a leader in a way that I could never be, but it did cross my mind at this point that I was abbot of this monastery, and had oversight and pastoral care of those who came here.

'No, I don't think so,' I said. 'Like Tear-Sing said, I think we've all listened to you enough.'

'Come!'

'I think I'd prefer to be with Tear-Sing at this time.'

'Why?'

'*Why?* Because you just killed him, that's why. You killed his bird. You killed Sanjay and now you've killed *him.*'

'*Come!*'

Was this my end? To be taken into the refectory and shot? Back of the head. That was the way. We went inside. And I remembered my father appearing after one of his long absences and me not quite knowing what to do or how to relate, and especially what to do with my hands and whether I was to kiss him, and I wanted to cry but I wanted to be pleased for him as well, and I wondered if it might be like that with God when we met, and I was glad that they said you didn't hear the gunshot that killed you.

'I wanted you to see,' said Skarit.

The darkness of the refectory always took a while to lighten. Tear-Sing had turned this darkness to advantage, with beautiful use of the candles. Had. He wouldn't now. But he *had*. Slowly, though, my eyes began to see. They saw the splintered cage and the ripped and splattered body of the rat.

'He is dead,' said Skarit.

'And Tear-Sing?'

'Only sleeping. Shock. Nothing more.'

*

I was at last alone and behind my study desk. It felt very good. It wasn't about power or status. They're as weak-kneed and fraudulent as each other. No, it was about protection. A protected place in which to reflect, sift and seek sense. It was a favour I had asked of Skarit and he had agreed. There was a different atmosphere in the place now. Hard to pin down. But it was different. Could I then evict the soldiers with their backgammon? Yes. So I had. And so I sat. Just sat, and delighted in it.

I contemplated the Sydney Opera House, and wondered what their experience of ladders, fascia work and pipe organs was, simulated or otherwise. And then my eyes drifted to the Sydney skyline and more particularly to the gaps. Seven of them. But now was not the time – not the time to fill them in, to bring the thing to completion. I hadn't quite got there. Completing a jigsaw is a very holy moment. It needs its own special time. I'd know the moment when it came. But it hadn't come yet. Not quite. There were certain matters pending, seeking resolution. And so the gaps remained, slightly upset no doubt by my apparent lack of concern, and I wandered over to the window searching inside for a deep thought, for the cobalt-blue revelation cut from the very centre of the earth and delivered by an angel of God.

I sat down again and noticed the letter for the first time. Or rather, the envelope containing the letter. The third letter. I had heard there were three letters and now knew the contents of the other two. One from Donaldo announcing his arrival. One for Carol from Lambeth Palace. But this one was mine. This was *my* letter. This was the one that stirred my little world. For unless I was very much mistaken, this would be the letter revealing the decision reached on the future of St James the Less.

I wasn't sure when it had been put there. But here it was, an arm-stretch away, and waiting on my pleasure. What was I hoping for? I was hoping for a decision, I suppose. Yes, it would be nice to know one way or another. There's a turbulence in uncertainty, in the unknowing, in the pending. Trouble is, as one pend disappears another ten pends seem to appear to replace it. Maybe the secret lies not in trying to exorcise all the pending parts of my life, but looking at the turbulence they cause and grasping the nettle of my illusion that I am in control of my destiny.

Still, that could wait, pending investigation. For the moment, resolution. I picked up the envelope. There was a knock on the door.

'Hello!' I shouted to whoever stood behind it. 'Come in!'

And Tear-Sing did. I put the letter down and smiled.

'I'm leaving shortly.'

'Fine. Where will you be going?'

'New York.'

'The Big –'

'Bernadette calls it the Big *Pear*.'

'Near enough.'

'Yes.'

Pause.

'It hasn't been an easy time for me here.'

'No. Well, I'm sorry. Genuinely sorry. Sorry that the earth hasn't moved for you. Or the sky opened for you. Ladders have been conspicuous by their absence, both in a physical and metaphysical sense.'

'That is not so, in fact.'

'Do you want to sit down?' I asked, bowled over by my momentary sense of concern for the well-being of a human other than myself. Shock waves in heaven.

'No, I'm not staying long. And I don't really want to talk now. But suffice to say that I have experienced something which for me is important and profound. *Solus ad solum.* Alone to the alone. You talked of that.'

'Did I? I'm sorry.'

'No, it was good. When Skarit carried me from the refectory today it was as though I was alone to the alone.'

My mind went back to the limp body, strongly held.

'I was held by one who is stronger than I,' continued Tear-Sing. 'I was held. I was safe. It was enough. It was beyond me but it was strong. And in its own way, it loved. Loved me. I was alone but not alone. I felt the imprint of God in my soul.'

'Well I thought God turning up in a stable was stretching things, but in Skarit's arms? Has our Lord got *no* shame?'

I was trying to deflate the intensity but Tear-Sing had no wish to. He needed to say what he had to, and so moved briskly on.

'There's a song sung by an American duo. Two women. You won't know them.[12] But in the song, they reflect on the emptiness of receiving the praise of strangers, but ending up alone. It has always haunted me. It probably always will. But it will not, I feel, be a bleak haunting from now on. Melancholic, but not bleak. Time will tell, but that is what I feel now. I'm not alone. And it's possible I may even be understood.'

'I see.'

'I am Tear-Sing the Sad, I always will be. But my sadness can contain joy and it can contain hope. Sometimes. In other words, it is not maybe the end of the story.'

'I'm glad for you.'

'I've said more than I meant to.'

'People always do.'

'I must go now.'

'Can I pray for you?'

'I don't think I want that at the moment.'

'No. Well, peace be with you anyway. Peace be with you out there, Tear-Sing, and may you be Jesus-Strong amid it all, who though rejected and misunderstood by family, village, clergy and disciples alike, never drifted into self-pity or Only-I-Exist demands, but kept to the path, held to the Way, in submission to his Father's will; who chose to say, amid all the crap, *thy* will be done. It's your line, Tear-Sing. Remember it amid the catwalks of New York. Thy will be done. And may Hope, Grace and Intimacy be yours. The Hope which knows a tomorrow; the Grace which declares the war over; and the Intimacy which feels the coming home.'

It was a hard-edged dismissal, brisk and businesslike but then that had seemed to be the nature of the encounter. It wasn't an emotional departure as our two ways parted, probably for eternity. There was much unspoken, much left unsaid. A short bow of his head, and Tear-Sing was gone. Back to the Big Banana. Back to his exquisite creations. Back to the strong arms of God which held and said, 'This is my beloved Son in whom I am deeply pleased.'

*

I contemplated the envelope. The handwriting and postal stamp were very familiar, as was the rich and thick 100-gram paper, with watermark. And once again, I applauded the efficiency of our Mother House. I'd known the decision was taken last week. It was gracious of them to communicate the result so quickly. Along with mass genocide and Christian calendars, inefficiency in the simple business of letting people know is a terrible crime against humanity, warranting if not hell, at least delayed arrival in the heavenly city due to paperwork being mislaid or no one being that bothered, frankly. Let the punishment fit the crime.

Still, enough uncertainty. We'll leave that for the saints. They can live with it. I can't. I reached for the envelope. There was a knock on the door.

'Hello!' I said. 'Come in!'

It was Carol. I put the envelope down and laughed.

'I'm not staying but I wanted to show you this.'

She held out a letter. I took it. Large girlish handwriting and a pleasure to read. Let's hope the Archbishop of Canterbury felt a similar sensation when he read it, for it was destined for the dizzy heights of Lambeth Palace.

'It's my reply.'

'Yes.'

It was brief and to the point. Yes, Carol was delighted to accept the Archbishop's offer. She felt humbled by the approach but excited by the challenge, and within the grace of God, she would do all in her power to bring the work of the commission to a conclusion which brought glory to God and new life to his Church. She'd obviously written acceptances before.

'It's my second draft.'

'Well, it's a very professional job. You certainly know all the right buttons to press. It's balancing the "How surprised I was to be considered" humility bit with the "Yes, I'm big enough and confident enough to handle this one, frankly" leadership bit. And, of course, managing to get *God* in as well. As I say, a very professional job.'

'Have you finished?'

'Sorry?'

'Its my second draft because my first draft said no.'

'Oh, I see. So it's a rethink, not a rewrite.'

'Indeed. Because I had decided against the commission. In fact, don't laugh –'

'There's little hope of that at the moment –'

'– but I *was* going to approach you about developing a home here for those experiencing Alzeimer's.'

'Now there's an idea.'

'I was going to offer to take it on. Spending time with Constantino –'

'Motivation? Apart from the obvious worthiness of it all.'

'Penance, probably.'

'Yes.'

'In the absence of anyone to beat me with a stick.'

My mind returned to Skarit's savage history lesson and Lawrence's last days.

'So what brought the change?'

'The blood. The mess. This afternoon – it was all right. I was covered in all-sorts this afternoon. I was Constantino's handkerchief for an hour. The rat's innards were almost secondary, compared to what comes out of him. And it didn't matter. There was really a wonderful sense of freedom in it all which I still haven't quite fathomed. But it was something about not having to be perfect or appear perfect any longer.'

'They do say that the moment of conversion comes for each of us when we are no longer able to maintain the image of ourselves which once contented us.'

'Well that's as maybe, but along with that freedom came the freedom to say yes to the Archbishop. If you know what I mean!'

I enjoyed the innuendo, particularly because it came from Carol, and seemed to confirm the stirrings of a glimmer of freedom and lightness within. A sense of inner laughter is particularly good for all the Carols out there.

'And what do you want?'

Carol's question caught me unawares.

'Sorry?'

'What do you want? You seem to know what everyone else wants. So what do *you* want?'

'What do I want? That would be telling.'

'Is that so hard?'

'Yes. And anyway, I don't know what everyone *wants.*'

'You pretend to then.'

'No. No I don't. I know what they *need.* There's a difference. What they need is that which will help them survive better. It's intermediate stuff. It's preparation for glory but not the glory itself. Joy and glory – or what people *want* – those are the concerns of the Dream-maker. Not my department at all. The longings, the yearnings, the wants, the hopes and fears of all those years – God. That's God's business. I'm just a place they must pass through on the way.'

'So what do *you* want?'

'I want to cry, I think. I'd like to cry. Feel the hot, wet, salty release down my cheeks. I'd like to sob. Yes, I think so. And, amid the release, scream love into eternity and hear not an echo but a reply.'

Pause.

'So you don't want a bishopric then?' ventured Carol tentatively.

'I'd prefer sex, frankly.'

'I see.'

'And if I can't have that, at least a hug.'

'Well, I can offer you that.'

And she did. A desert hug. I felt the warmth.

'And tell me something,' I said, 'because I'm a nosy old so-and-so sometimes. When you shouted at Tear-Sing to "give it to him" – what did you mean?'

'What do you think?'

'I think I think that you were telling him to hand the gun over.'

This time it was Carol who smiled.

'Wrong. I meant him to shoot Skarit. I was very angry. It just all came to the surface. I couldn't believe I was saying it, but I was saying it, and meaning it. I was telling him to kill. Why do you ask?'

'No reason. As I say, I was just being nosy. We do different things on the edge of the universe, I suppose. Things we wouldn't allow ourselves to do at home.'

And then the bell. A pretty pathetic threadbare sound, but enough to call us to prayer.

'I'll accompany you down to the chapel, and pray particularly that no one upsets you in your new post. Shootings on the liturgical commission could seriously damage your career.'

It was a slightly risky joke, but she took it in good part. She didn't exactly fall off her chair in rib-aching mirth, but it was okay. She smiled again. Things had indeed changed.

So we left Brother Gun and Sister Jigsaw and climbed down the narrow staircase which led out into the courtyard. Let us pray.

*

What do I remember from that evening? Fragments only, I'm afraid. I remember the ladder certainly. It was stunning, as was the simple cloth backdrop taking all of us gathered in the chapel so simply yet so vividly back to Jacob's dream and the heavens opened. It was Tear-Sing's farewell gift. Not Ted's. Ted the Yes had apparently left that afternoon, without a goodbye. So Tear-Sing had made the ladder himself, leaving a note saying: 'Don't rule out the angels.'

And I remember Donaldo whispering in my ear shortly before we started that he would be Donaldo the Duck from here on. Another humility stunt? It didn't sound like it, but I couldn't be sure. And I remember being hit by the line in the Lord's Prayer, 'Give us today our daily bread.' It invited me, Peter the Fool, to give up trying to understand everything and live simply for the day. I needed the world to stop instantly so I could confess.

And I remember believing. Yes, I remember that well, because obviously it doesn't happen very often. I remember believing as I dismissed everyone with the words that the message of Jesus was that the war is over. Our weapons cupboards – they can be emptied. Our defence mechanisms can be cast aside. God is our friend, inviting us from the straitjacket of our past into a future where things which were not sung to us in our cradle become possible.

In the silence that followed, I pondered my own cradle songs; the little person who was me, aged eight, in a stripy orange and white shirt, crying, struggling, laughing, fighting, hoping. And I held out my hand to this fat little boy because I liked him. We walked and talked, little and large. We were friends. I think I'd forgotten that somewhere along the way. Continuity with the past is not just about giving saints haloes. It's about giving our little selves haloes. And I resolved then that we'd meet again. Didn't know where, didn't know when. But I knew we'd meet again some sunny day. Or indeed, some cloudy one. The weather was irrelevant – the meeting, everything …

*

And I remember a conversation with Skarit. Throughout the evening office, he'd inhabited the shadows in the chapel. Afterwards, as people slowly left and I extinguished the candles, he approached me.

'You called me a liar yesterday. After the incident with Constantino and the boys. I said it was about discipline. And you called me a liar. People don't say that to me. Why did you say it?'

'Because you were – you were a liar. You were lying. Is that clear enough an answer?'

'What do you mean?'

'I mean that you were a good man yesterday. You called Faust's bluff. I don't think it was just about discipline. I think you intervened on behalf of the defenceless. I think you were strong for the weak, which of course is what you were made for.'

His big eyes looked away. This was not a story or an idea which had been sung to him in *his* cradle. He breathed deeply from his chest, and then turned to look at me again.

'I cannot become as you.'

'That's the last thing I'd want, or the world needs.'

'But Muhammad did say that there was nothing more powerful than a fairy tale in the mouth of a wise man. I like your fairy tale.'

'It's a good story, isn't it?'

'It is, yes.'

We walked gently and silently across the courtyard. We passed the gallows, where Sanjay had twisted and Dalip had pulled. We passed the spot where Tear-Sing's bird had been ripped to pieces, and where Sanjay had raised his arm in defiance. We skirted the site of Constantino's humiliation and Skarit's mock execution of the young soldier. Finally, we stood where Tear-Sing had been held and laid.

'Yes, it really is a very good story,' I said. A very good story indeed. Unless, of course –'

'Unless what?'

'Unless you're a rat.'

'The rat is dead, Abbot Peter.'

'Yes. The rat is dead, Skarit. Long live the rat.'

*

The jigsaw was waiting for me. So patient. And now was the time. The holy moment had arrived. The few remaining pieces were slowly but enjoyably placed. I sealed the Sydney sky. I plugged the holes in the heavens. I was exhausted by the heavens being quite so open frankly – Jacob's, Sydney's, and ours. Exhilarated but exhausted. I was bringing a little order to things. And a sense of completion. Which just left the envelope …

Once again, I picked it up. I waited for the knock on the door. It didn't come. I was a little disappointed. I feared the contents, I think. I looked for the knife, cut the cream envelope and pulled out an invoice for building work to St James which had wrongly been sent to our Mother House. They werc kindly sending it on. Thank you. Give us today our daily bread, as they say. For the moment, I didn't need to know more. There was a sort of a joy to be found here. The ascent to nought. Desert ascent.

Editor's Notes

1 Though Abbot Peter would have us believe that he's a shuffling and decrepit ninety-three years old, my own research leads me to believe that he is in fact about sixty-one. That, at least, is what the warden at Horace Gardens Day Centre told me.

2 He does go *on* about this, as you will see. Wouldn't want him in my congregation. He'd sit there in silence. But *everything* would be a problem, and not quite as good as it used to be in the desert.

3 Those unversed in pompous Anglican newspapers may not have heard of the *Church Times*. But it is the Anglican paper of record, read avidly by clergy. It is read particularly avidly by those looking to change job. This explains its very large circulation.

4 1 Corinthians 13:12. Paul bravely admits to

knowing a good deal less than everything. The Good News version has it as a 'dim image in a mirror' which well describes the reflection of a number of people I know.

5 'The ascent to nought' is a classic description of our spiritual journey in the writings of the Christian mystics. Abbot Peter doesn't seem bothered enough to explain it, and Carol duly misunderstands him, I think. She seems to equate it with becoming a doormat. This is not so. Put simply, there is a good nought and a bad nought, and it is important to distinguish between the two, for they are very different creatures.

The bad nought is being treated as nothing; being set at nought by others and ignored or abused accordingly. There is no health here. There is no God here. Just damage and scars, which some people must struggle with all their lives.

The nought talked of by the mystics, however, is a very different animal. It is a happy, amazed and rather merry nought. It is an incredulous nought born out of a growing awareness that I am loved by God above all things, yet still completely unable to answer the question *why?* Anyway, it is so, God be praised and, consequently, vanity and affectation flee away in this glorious nakedness before the Divine. And a very happy sense of nought is arrived at. Evelyn Underhill describes these things well. But then she describes most things well.

6 Genesis 28:10–19.

7 Abbot Peter seems to want to have it both ways. One moment he's telling us that 'conventional wisdom sucks'. The next, he's waxing lyrical about being in deep communion with the past. This maybe something he needs to work through with his therapist. Maybe he's tried and the therapist fell asleep.

8 Abbot Peter either got an Alice Miller book for Christmas or would enjoy one. She talks about Stalin as well. She's also very interesting on why Buster Keaton could never smile in public. But with Alice Miller, parents be warned. She has rasping things to say to those given the care of children.

9 This explains Skarit's surprising command of English which had been puzzling me. Amid the decline of our football, cricket and other sports too numerous to mention on the international stage, it is reassuring to know that we can still

train (and indeed *arm*) a decent despot. Gold medals and bubbly all round, I think, and three cheers for government funding.

10 John 8:3–11. Only recorded in the gospel of John and, even there, it's in brackets and always accompanied by mealy-mouthed comments about these verses 'not being in the best manuscripts'. Of course not. No one could quite believe Jesus would do and say such a thing, which makes me believe it's probably the most authentic story from his life which we have on record. That's enough textual criticism, however. Any more and this book is in danger of appearing in a theological college library, which would really be very sad.

11 Isaiah 64:1

12 The band is the Indigo Girls. Haven't yet traced the song, but am enjoying the search.